"What specifically is bothering you?"

She watched his mouth move as he said the words. His lips looked soft, the slight edge of whiskers around them only serving to outline their manly shape. "It's…it's the kiss," she heard herself blurt. "Maybe I've forgotten how."

Heat washed up her cheeks. It was thinking of him, his mouth, his tongue, his taste that was rattling her brain and tripping up her pulse.

His grip tightened, just those two fingers making her immobile, keeping her captured as he bent close. "Then let me remind you," he whispered, his breath warm against her face, "of exactly how two pairs of lips are supposed to meet."

Dear Reader,

Last week, our neighbors' daughter visited and I held her newborn in my arms. I felt both protective and enchanted of her sweet warmth and it brought me instantly back to my days as a babysitter when I was a young teen. Oh, the nights I spent with kids not my own! The diapers changed, the owies kissed, the way those little people burrowed into my young heart.

I was reminded again that I'm a sucker for kids of all sizes.

So is Kayla James, the nanny for eleven-year-old Jane and eight-year-old Lee. She's been with them since their mom died six years before and somewhere in those six years she's also fallen for their father, firefighter Mick Hanson. But will the widower ever look at her as someone other than his children's caregiver?

For Mick's part, he knows he's attracted to the pretty woman who shares his kids and his kitchen, but he's uncertain he can take on another person's happiness. The man's forgotten that the head cannot always rule the heart, and this good guy will be reminded of this fact while also dealing with the normal events of family life.

Some of those events come straight from my world... hope you enjoy a glimpse of my real-life cat, Goblin, and my husband's Impossible Football Catch, not to mention grilled cheese-and-pickle-relish (yuck!) sandwiches for breakfast.

Best wishes,

Christie Ridgway

NOT JUST THE NANNY

CHRISTIE RIDGWAY

SPECIAL EDITION®

Published by Silhouette Books

America's Publisher of Contemporary Romance

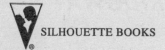 SILHOUETTE BOOKS

Recycling programs
for this product may
not exist in your area.

ISBN-13: 978-0-373-65558-8

NOT JUST THE NANNY

Copyright © 2010 by Christie Ridgway

Books by Christie Ridgway

Silhouette Special Edition

Beginning with Baby #1315
From This Day Forward #1388
*In Love with Her Boss #1441
Mad Enough to Marry #1481
Bachelor Boss #1895
I Still Do #1950
Runaway Bride Returns! #1973

Silhouette Desire

His Forbidden Fiancée #1791

Silhouette Yours Truly

The Wedding Date
Follow That Groom!
Have Baby, Will Marry
Ready, Set...Baby!
Big Bad Dad
The Millionaire and the Pregnant Pauper

*Montana Mavericks: Home for the Holidays

CHRISTIE RIDGWAY

Native Californian Christie Ridgway started reading and writing romances in middle school. It wasn't until she was the wife of her college sweetheart and the mother of two small sons that she submitted her work for publication. Many contemporary romances later, she is the happiest when telling her stories despite the splash of kids in the pool, the mass of cups and plates in the kitchen and the many commitments she makes in the world beyond her desk.

Besides loving the men in her life and her dream-come-true job, she continues her longtime love affair with reading and is never without a stack of books. You can find out more about Christie at her Web site, www.christieridgway.com.

For all those who've given their heart to a child
not their own.

Chapter One

The woman on the sofa beside Kayla James suddenly sat up straight and looked at her with round eyes. "I've got it. I've finally figured out why you've been turning down men and declining invitations. You... you've broken the cardinal rule of nannies!"

Kayla ignored the flush racing over her face and focused on the bowl of pretzels sitting on the coffee table. "I don't know what you're talking about."

"Oh, yes, you do," Betsy Sherbourne said. Her long, dark hair was pulled back in a ponytail and she looked barely old enough to be a mother's helper, let alone a full-fledged fellow nanny. She wiggled, bouncing the ruby-colored cushions. "You know exactly what I'm talking about."

Kayla pulled the edges of her oversized flannel shirt together. There was a chill in the air tonight. "You're jumping to conclusions because I didn't feel like being the fourth in your blind double date last weekend."

"The fact is, you haven't gone anywhere in months," Betsy replied. "Your social life is limited to these weeknight, girls-only get-togethers we have with our friends from the nanny service."

Kayla latched on to the new topic like a lifeline. "Did I tell you that the others can't come tonight? Everybody had a conflict except Gwen, who should be here any minute," she said, naming the woman who owned and ran the We ♥ Our Nanny service which had placed both Kayla and Betsy with their current families.

"Yes, you told me," Betsy said. "And I won't let you change the subject."

"Look," Kayla responded, feeling a little desperate. "You know I'm busy with my job and school."

"Half of that's not an excuse you can use anymore."

Kayla sighed. Her friend was right. A couple months back she'd finally been awarded her college degree at the advanced age of almost twenty-seven.

Since then, her friends had bombarded her with suggestions about how to fill her newfound free time. "I should have never let you guys throw me that graduation party," she grumbled.

"Yeah, and other than those brief hours when we whooped it up, when was the last time you took some time out for yourself?"

"Today. I went shopping. I bought bras." Kayla rummaged in the knitting basket beside her, withdrawing the almost-finished mitten she was working on. "What do you think?" she asked in a bright voice, still determined to distract her friend. "Is this large enough for Lee? He's big for eight."

"Bras?" Sounding skeptical, Betsy ignored the mention of Lee, one of the two children Kayla looked after. "What color bras?"

"What does color have to do with anything?"

There was pity in the other woman's gaze. "Kayla, swear to me you have more than white cotton in your lingerie drawer."

She felt her cheeks go hot again. "Do we really have to—"

"Okay." Betsy relented. "Just tell me about these bras, then."

"The bras. They…" Kayla sighed again. "Okay, fine. They were for Jane."

"Jane! Jane's first bras?"

Kayla nodded, hope kindling that this would be the topic to derail the original discussion, even though it was a risk to bring up the kids again, as the second cardinal rule of nannies was to never get too attached to the children. "Can you believe it? All her friends have them now. Time has sure flown."

"Yes." Betsy reached for a pretzel and eyed Kayla again. "And you've given Mick and his kids almost six undivided years of yours now."

Uh-oh. She was losing the battle once more. "I've not *given* it to them," Kayla said, aware she sounded defensive. "I've been *employed* by Mick to take care of his daughter and son." It had been ideal. As a fire-fighter, after his wife died in a car accident, Mick had needed an overnight, in-house adult when he was on a twenty-four-hour shift. His schedule, however, had enough off-duty time in it that Kayla could pursue her degree part-time. But now that she'd graduated, and now that the kids were getting older, eleven and eight, the people in her circle were starting to squawk about Kayla making some adjustments.

Heavy footsteps sounded on the stairs. "La-La," a voice called from above. Mick's voice, using the name that toddler Lee had used for Kayla when she'd first come to live with them.

Jumping to her feet, she strode to the bottom of the staircase, her expression determinedly blank in case her nosy friend was watching her too closely. "You rang, boss?" she asked, focusing on his descending shoes since no one would show inconvenient emotion staring at shoelaces. His feet stopped moving at the bottom of the steps. She detected his just-out-of-the-shower scent now, and she put the back of her fingers to her nose in order not to inhale it too deeply. The soap-on-a-rope and companion aftershave had been her Christmas present to him and she should have thought twice before purchasing a fragrance that appealed to her so much.

"Hey, there, Betsy," he called over Kayla's head. "I'll be out of the way of you ladies in a minute." His voice lowered. "Can I talk to you in the kitchen?"

She glanced up. She shouldn't have.

When had it happened? When exactly had the widower she'd first met, the man with five o'clock shadow and weary eyes, gone from gaunt to gorgeous? The straight, dark hair hadn't changed, but he smiled now. There was warm humor more often than not in his deep brown eyes. She supposed he still had his demons—she knew he did, because on occasion she'd catch him sitting in the darkened living room staring off into space. But he'd found a way to manage his grief and be a good dad to his kids.

A good man.

One who looked at her, who treated her, just as

if Kayla was the fifteen-year-old girl next door who occasionally babysat when both she and Mick had to be out.

She followed him across the hardwood floor, trying not to ogle the way his jeans fit his lean hips or how his shoulders filled out the simple sport shirt. She'd ironed it for him as part of her job, of course, just as she'd helped Jane pick it out as his Christmas gift, knowing the soft chamois color would look wonderful with his olive skin.

In the kitchen, he swung around, nearly catching her too-interested examination. He was only thirty-four years old, but she figured he'd have a heart attack if he knew in which direction the nanny had been staring. With a flick of her lashes, she redirected her eyes to the calendar posted on the double-wide refrigerator that was nestled between oak cabinets and red-and-white-tiled countertops. Mick turned his head to follow her gaze.

"Okay," he said. "We're good, right? You've got your nanny service friends here tonight. Jane is working on her poetry project, but she's only two doors down and will walk herself home, after she calls so you can watch her from the front porch."

"Yep." They went through this routine every day. She didn't know if it was a result of Mick losing his wife in such a sudden way, if it was because he was a man trained for disasters, or just because he adored his children. All made perfect sense to her. "And Jared's mom will drive Lee home after Scouts."

"Bases covered, then." His mouth turned up in a rueful grin that she let herself enjoy from the corner of her eye. "So I really don't have any excuse not to meet the guys for pizza and a cold one or two."

"None that I can think of." She smiled, despite wondering if that "cold one with the guys" included a couple of hot women. He'd dated on occasion— well, he'd gone along with varying degrees of good grace when someone fixed him up—but she thought she'd detected in him a change there, too. A new tension that everything female in her suspected had to do with his growing need for opposite-gender adult companionship.

Something he surely didn't consider her in the running for.

He reached out and tugged on the ends of her blond hair in a manner that made that perfectly clear. Jane got the same treatment from him often enough.

"Why the sad eyes, La-La?"

She pinned on a second smile. "Just one of those days."

"Tell me about it." Mick shoved his hands in his pockets. "They're growing up, Kayla, and I can't tell you what a blow it was when Jane spilled about your shopping trip. All at once I felt about a hundred."

"Nonsense. You're only a few years older than I."

He shook his head. "Yeah, but today my little girl went to the mall where she bought…bought…" One hand slipped out of his pocket to make a vague gesture. "You know."

Amused by his inability to articulate, Kayla leaned nearer. "Bras, Mick," she whispered, a laugh in her voice. Her gaze lifted. "It's not a dirty word."

Their eyes met. *Oh,* she thought, as something sparked to life in his. Suddenly, more than humor seemed to warm them. With a soundless crack, heat flashed down her neck and the oxygen in the room turned desert-dry. She wanted to put out a hand to steady herself, but she was afraid whatever she touched would emit a jolting shock.

Bras? she thought. Dirty? Did one of those two words made it feel so…so naughty to be this close to him?

Mick blinked, severing the connection, then he turned away to grab a glass from the cupboard by the sink. With a steady hand, he filled it with water and took a long drink in a gesture so casual she figured she must have imagined that moment of…of… whatever.

Wishful thinking on her part?

Kayla cleared her throat and folded her arms over her chest, the shirt fluttering at her hips. Maybe if she wore something other than jeans and flannel around him, he might notice her. But he'd had years to do that—summers when she'd been in shorts and tank tops, vacations by a pool when she'd worn a swimsuit that wasn't *Sports Illustrated*–ready but that didn't cover her like a tent, either. He'd never appeared the slightest bit intrigued by any of it. When she'd recently cut twelve inches from her long hair he hadn't noticed for two weeks, and then only when someone else mentioned it.

Upon inspection of the new do, he'd appeared appalled by the change. She'd felt stupid, like that time he'd caught her about to bestow a good-night kiss on a date on the doorstep. The fact that she'd been glad of the interruption, and that afterward she'd daydreamed in her bed of Mick pulling her away from the other man and into his own arms instead, hadn't been good signs.

That event had occurred six months ago, and since then she hadn't dated anyone—or shown any interest in dating anyone—which had prompted Betsy's earlier conversation.

"Well," Mick said, pulling open the dishwasher

to rack his glass, "I guess I'll head out now. Have fun."

"You, too."

He strode toward the door that led to the garage, then hesitated. "Kayla," he said.

Her heart jumped. "Yes?"

"In case I've never said it…"

She held her breath.

"You're great. You've always been great." He swung around. Reached out. "Such a pal to me," he added, patting her shoulder.

Her skin jittered, his light touch zinging all the way through the heavy plaid fabric of her shirt.

No. Make that *his* shirt. She'd been attached to it like a new fiancée to her engagement ring since the last time she'd removed it from the dryer.

"Yeah." He patted her again. "Such a pal to me."

And as he walked away, the appreciative words slid down her throat like a medicinal dose of disappointment to land like lead at the bottom of her belly. Who knew that "such a pal to me" could cause such gloom?

But somehow it did, because…

Oh, boy. Oh, no. Oh, it was useless to deny the truth any longer.

Betsy was right, it seemed. Kayla *had* shattered

the number-one item on the no-no list. Because the cardinal rule of nannies was simple.

Never fall in love with the daddy.

It wasn't until the barmaid set the cold beer in front of Mick that he actually registered his surroundings. He looked around the place that should have been as familiar to him as the back of his hand. He'd been coming to O'Hurley's with his buddies Will, Austin and Owen for years.

"When the hell did they paint the walls?" he groused, scanning the cream-colored surface. "What was wrong with dingy gray?" Then he craned his neck to inspect the rest of the interior. "And new TVs? Were the other ones broken?"

Austin stared at him, his dark eyes perplexed. "Dude. Flat-screens. Each of 'em as big as the back end of my grandma's Buick. You'd rather watch the game on something smaller?"

Mick lifted his beer for a swallow. "I'd prefer things to stay just as they were," he mumbled.

Owen's brows rose. "Good God, Mick. You sound like a grumpy old man. Next you'll be yelling at kids to get off your lawn."

He felt like a grumpy old man. That was the problem. The store department he always averted his eyes from was now the new playground for his preteen daughter. His son was out of T-ball already. His nanny was a college graduate.

"The kids in my house are almost too old to play on the grass," he said. "Lee and Jane and Kayla are growing up before my eyes. I'm almost afraid to blink."

"Mick..." His friend and fellow firefighter Will Dailey wasn't blinking. He was staring, just like Austin had a few moments before. "Kayla's not a kid. You know that, right?"

"She's a student," he shot back. "That makes her a kid. Sort of." It sounded stupid even to his ears, but he could only afford to think of the nanny in those terms.

"I thought you told us she graduated. From college. And she's got to be in her mid-twenties."

Mick waved a hand. "Still a girl."

Austin grinned. "Looks like a woman to me. As a matter of fact—"

"She's off-limits," Mick ordered.

The other guys were staring again, so Mick jerked up his chin and focused on the television. "How about those Cowboys?"

"How about those cheerleaders?" Austin countered.

Which was exactly why Mick had warned the

other man off. He was all about the superficial stuff, flashy boots, short skirts, and big...pom poms.

"You can't keep them all under wraps forever," Will said quietly from his seat in the booth beside Mick. "Believe me. I raised my five younger brothers and sisters and among the many things I learned, besides how to stretch a dollar until it squeals for mercy, was that they grow up and then itch to get out on their own."

Mick groaned. "I don't want to think about that." It didn't take a genius to figure out why. After losing his wife, Ellen, and the future he'd envisioned for them had been snatched away so cruelly, he couldn't imagine how hard it would be for him to loosen his hold on his kids.

Will laughed a little. "Nature has a way of making that easier. It's called 'the teenage years.'"

"Yeah, I suppose." Mick took another swallow of his beer. "Though I've already explained to Jane there will be no dating until she's thirty-one."

Will laughed again. "Good luck with that. But maybe all this would be a little easier if you considered finding a love interest yourself."

"Not going to happen." He couldn't imagine it. Although life with Ellen had been good—despite the fact that they'd been so young he could hardly recognized the kid groom he'd been in the man he was now—he had no plans to add a permanent woman to his life. He barely managed his current situation. Single dad, fire captain and somehow a romantic relationship, too? Wasn't going to happen.

He couldn't take on the additional responsibility… he didn't *want* the responsibility, even for the tempting trade-off of regular companionship in his bed.

Not to mention the difficulty of finding someone the rest of his household would get along with, too. "What kind of woman would Jane and Lee like? And Kayla? Who would she approve of?"

"Mick, Kayla's the nanny. And she's not going to be with you forever anyway, right?"

Wrong.

No, no, not wrong. Kayla gone was just something else he couldn't picture in his head.

He had another image in there instead, one that had been impossible to banish, for the last six months. She'd been out for the evening and he'd just gotten Lee back to sleep after the third request for water when he'd heard a muffled thump coming from the porch. Without thinking, he'd yanked open the front door, only to find…to find…

It replayed in his mind. A young man, sporting a sandy crew cut, his hands cupped around Kayla's face, his mouth descending toward her upturned lips. The moment had stretched out, it seemed, forever.

Mick had time to notice the bright glint of Kayla's shiny blond hair in the lamplight, the dark sweep of her lashes against her cheek and then the stunning blue of her eyes as they lifted and she caught him witnessing her good-night moment.

They'd flared wide and her cheeks had flushed pink as she hastily stepped back from her date and away from the almost-kiss. "I…um…uh…" she'd said, her gaze fixed on Mick's.

Instead of smoothing the moment over and re-treating, Mick, bad Mick, had merely held the door open so she could slip inside. He supposed he'd been frowning, because it was the proper expression for a man feeling decidedly hot under the collar.

Like an overprotective father might feel.

Or a jealous—no!

But damn, ever since that night he hadn't been able to see her as "just" the nanny. Although she'd never been that, not with the way she'd taken to his children and they'd taken her into their hearts. But he hadn't seen her as a woman, a kissable, desirable, damn beautiful woman until that awkward instant on the porch.

And he hadn't been able to stop thinking about it for one day since, even though he didn't believe she'd seen that young man again, or any other in the six months that had passed.

She's not going to be with you forever anyway, right? Now it was Will's question on replay in his head. But damn it, she was with his family now, and he had a sudden compunction to return to his house, just to assure himself that she *was* still there and that everything else was also still the same.

Mick got to his feet and fished some bills from his pocket. Austin looked up. "Where you going?"

"I want to be home when Lee gets back from Scouts. I need to watch my daughter walk down the sidewalk." *I have to see that Kayla isn't kissing some man.*

He'd forgotten about her nanny friends, though. When he spotted their cars outside his house, he let himself into the kitchen through the back door and decided to make do with leftovers for dinner. The kids had already eaten and he'd run from the bar before the pizza they'd ordered with their beer had arrived.

Even with his head in the refrigerator, Mick could hear Kayla's voice rise. "All right, fine. You win."

Bemused by her beleaguered tone, he straightened. He strolled toward the doorway that led to the dining room and from there the living room, wondering if she needed him to distract her friends. It sounded as if they were on his pretty Kayla's case about something.

No. Not his Kayla. Remember that. Not. His. Kayla.

She spoke again. "I said I'll do it."

"You agree?" It was her friend Betsy's voice.

"That's what I said," she answered, sounding testy.

Poor girl. He took another step closer to the living room. He could picture Kayla's flushed cheeks, her silky blond hair mussed by frustrated fingers. Her eyes, surrounded by her long, dark brown lashes, would stand out like blue jewels as she gazed on her friends.

"You'll go on the date?"

Mick froze.

"I've got to do something," he heard his nanny mutter. "So, yes."

If there was more conversation from the living room, Mick didn't hear it, not when he was contemplating just why her need to "do something" had turned into a need to date. Not when he was wondering exactly how many front-porch kisses that would mean.

Not when he was considering if he could manage to interrupt every single one of them.

His footsteps retreated back toward the refrigerator as resignation settled over him. Kayla. Back to dating? Damn. And double damn.

Despite his best hopes, it appeared as if he was going to be forced into doing some kissing himself. As in kissing his status quo goodbye.

Chapter Two

Kayla's bedroom and bath were located down a short hallway off the kitchen, while the rest of the household slept upstairs. And they were still at it the morning after her nanny group get-together, which gave her time to stew alone while the coffee brewed. Both she and Mick liked theirs medium strong, but hot, hot, hot. After an internet search, last Christmas he'd located a new maker that he'd wrapped and placed under the tree. It had been tagged to both of them, from "Santa Starbucks."

Funny man.

But not the man she should be thinking about at the moment. A normal, non-rule-breaking nanny should be contemplating the double date she'd agreed to let Betsy set up—the other woman had an address book full of eligibles, apparently. Lord knew that Mick—the widower who wouldn't see her as a woman—wasn't one of those. She sighed.

Then sighed again, because darn it, she was thinking about him again when the only sensible thing to do was forget all about the man—or at least find a way to dispatch these inconvenient feelings she had for him.

Determined to put Mick from her head, she pulled a coffee mug from the cupboard and then directed her gaze to the window over the sink. It looked out onto the backyard patio, the sprawling oak beside it, and then the rectangular expanse of grass. Two sections of fencing had been removed to facilitate the neighbors' pool building. Like every morning for the last week, a good-looking man tramped around the area, taking notes on a yellow pad.

Pool contractor. A definitely good-looking one in that way of men who worked outdoors. His hair was breeze-tousled, the ends lightened by the sun. His face and forearms were tanned and the rest of him looked fit and strong.

As she watched, he turned and caught her eye through the window then gestured for her to come outside. Her heartbeat ticked up a little as she stepped through the sliding door that led to the back. They'd had a few conversations and she'd found him pleasant. Friendly. Betsy would place him squarely in the eligible category. "Hey, Pete," she called. "Everything okay?"

"I just wanted to let you know we'll have the fence back up on Monday." He paused to give her a smile. "How are you this morning?"

"Good." She smiled back. "Fine."

"And the kids?"

"Terrific." It struck her that a woman who didn't have a thing for the firefighter who signed her paychecks would be clearing something up for Eligible Pete about right now. So… "You know, um, Jane and Lee, they're not *my* kids."

"Oh, I got that," he assured her. "You're too young to be their mother."

She frowned at that. Technically, not true. "Well—"

"I was raised by a stepmom myself. Love the woman to pieces, even more for taking on the ragtag rowdies that were me and my little brothers."

They had something in common, she thought. "I have stepparents myself."

"A split in your family, too?"

"When I was ten. Both parents married other people, had more kids." Leaving her the lonely-only issue of their short-term union. Now her mother and father had big rambunctious families with their new spouses.

"That must make it crazy on Christmas and Thanksgiving for you."

She forced a laugh. "Sure." More often than not, though, each parent assumed the other had set Kayla a place at their table—which left her with no place at all.

"Yeah," Pete spoke again. "All that blended family business must mean you and Mick have a lot to juggle." His gaze shifted over her shoulder.

Kayla turned to see what had snagged the pool contractor's attention. Who. Mick. Coffee in hand, he was eyeing them out the window. Even from here she could detect the comb lines in his just-shampooed hair. The man liked his showers.

And just like that, her memory kicked in and she swore she could smell the scent of his damp skin. Her hands tightened on her mug as a little shiver tracked down her spine. She really shouldn't have gifted him with that delicious aftershave.

"How long have you two been together?"

"Six years," Kayla murmured absently, her mind still far away. When Mick returned home from work, he almost always made a stop in the laundry room on the first floor where he stripped off his boots, socks and shirt. If she could get away with it undetected, she'd watch him walk through the kitchen and then up the stairs bare-chested, the muscles in his back shifting with every footstep. There were a lot of those muscles—all along his spine and across his shoulders, although she particularly liked the ones that moved so subtly at the small of his back, right above the taut rise of his—

Pete's question suddenly sank in. *How long have you two been together?*

She whipped back to face the contractor. "Oh. Oh, no. Mick and I… We're not together."

"You don't live together?" Pete asked, his expression perplexed.

"Well, yes, obviously we live together, but we don't, um, *live together.* I'm just the nanny to his children. To Jane and Lee."

"Oh." Pete's confusion seemed to intensify. "He didn't mention that."

Kayla frowned. "You were talking about me to Mick?"

Pete gave her a wry smile. "Just trying to get the lay of the land, if you know what I mean."

He'd been asking about her? If Betsy was here, she'd be thrilled by the news. Kayla realized she only felt embarrassed. "I suppose I do."

"And Mick gave me the impression that the, uh, land was, already, uh...uh..."

She glanced at the house, then looked at Pete again. "Already, uh...uh...what?"

"I probably misunderstood," Pete answered quickly. "I asked for your cell phone number and he got this weird expression on his face."

She frowned. "What kind of weird expression?"

Pete hesitated. "The kind that made clear your evenings weren't free."

A burn shot up her neck. More embarrassment. Maybe irritation. Likely an uncomfortable combination of the two. Mick was warning men off from her—even though he didn't seem to notice she was even a girl?

Such a pal to me.

"It must have been a misunderstanding," Pete started. "Though I..."

Kayla didn't hear the rest of what he had to say, as she was already stalking back to the house. What right did Mick have to interfere? she fumed, her temper kindling. He'd already invaded her nightly dreams. Wasn't that enough for him?

She flung back the sliding door and stomped into the kitchen. The man she worked for looked up from the utensil drawer he was rummaging through. "Was that guy bugging you?" he demanded.

"No!" She frowned, even as she noticed he looked handsomer and fitter and stronger than the pool contractor she'd left outside. His jeans and faded sweatshirt were nothing special, so the eye was drawn to the masculine angles of his face. He was all guy, from his midnight-black bristly lashes to the scuffed toes of his running shoes. And all-out attractive, she thought, then shoved it from her mind as she remembered she was mad at him. "Bugging me is—"

"Kayla," wailed Jane from the doorway. "What will I do? I can't go to school like this."

Kayla whirled toward the preteen, saw the distress on her face and then the outstretched fingernails with their messily applied raspberry-colored polish. "Oh, Jane," she said, hurrying toward her. "Don't worry. We can clean them off in a jiffy."

"No." Tragedy laced the single word and was written all over the eleven-year-old's face. *"Every* girl is coming to school with their nails painted today."

Kayla glanced at Mick and took in his baffled expression. "Jane," he said. "It's no big deal. Let Kayla help you take all that junk off and—"

"I have an even better idea," Kayla said, widening her eyes at her employer to signal that he was an uninformed male moment away from a true crisis. "In my bathroom is this great little tool shaped like a marking pen that erases polish gone awry. Your nails will look perfect in five minutes."

It was more like ten, but when Jane returned to the kitchen with Kayla, she was all smiles. "Look, Daddy," she said, fanning her fingers for her father's eyes. "See how pretty they look."

Mick obediently bent for an inspection. Jane didn't appear to notice, but Kayla saw the dismay that washed over his face. Then he looked over his daughter's head to meet her eyes and she knew what he was thinking.

First bras. Painted fingernails. What was next? Jane was moving from little girl to young woman one morning at a time and he could do nothing to stop the transition. Even though she was still mad at him, Kayla moved toward father and daughter, and brushed Jane's hair behind her shoulder.

"Remember those spa sleepovers we used to throw, Janie?" she asked. "Your friends would come over and I'd paint all your nails with glitter polish and put avocado masks on your faces." She glanced at Mick, projecting the message that the same little girl who ran around in Disney princess pajamas and bunny slippers was still inside this growing child with her long, coltish legs and slender fingers.

"We should do that again," Jane said, turning to Kayla with eagerness.

"It would be fun," she agreed.

"And not just fingernail polish and facial masks," Jane insisted. "We'll also try—" her voice lowered with reverence "—makeup."

Kayla glanced at Mick again, catching his wince. *Makeup,* he mouthed over his daughter's head. *Makeup!*

She smiled at him, both amused and sympathetic. "Don't let it get you down, big guy."

He smiled back, his gaze wry and warm and so intimate that it was as if they were touching palm to palm. The sensation traveled up her arm to her chest where it wrapped around her heart. And she could read his mind again. He was thinking—

"Let's do it soon," Jane said, her voice breaking that bond between her father and Kayla. "Say we can do it tonight. It's Friday."

Kayla started. *Tonight!* She remembered what she'd already agreed to do this weekend. "Maybe the next one? I have a date, Jane." A double date with Betsy and the two eligibles. A social event she hoped would get her mind and heart off Mick, she thought with a frown.

Something that so far she hadn't managed for more than two minutes at a time.

* * *

Mick didn't consider himself an expert on females, not by any means. Take his daughter, for example. Her moods swayed with the breeze and made no sense to him at all. But Kayla...sometimes they'd share a glance or a smile and he swore he could see straight through her.

And right now she didn't seem too happy about that date she'd set up last night.

Strange how that seemed to put him, on the other hand, in a sudden good mood. "What's the matter, La-La?" he asked as he passed her on the way to the refrigerator. Like him, she was dressed casually in jeans, running shoes and a sweatshirt that read Mary Poppins Rocks. "Is it—"

He was interrupted by the arrival of his son, Lee, in the kitchen, looking half-awake in his San Francisco 49ers flannel pajamas and with his dark hair sticking straight up in the back, his brown eyes at half-mast. With zombie footsteps, he walked over to Kayla and simply leaned into her, as if he was no longer able to stand on his own.

She held him against her, her palm smoothing the boy's porcupine hair. "Morning, sleepy."

"Morning, La-La," Lee murmured.

Mick couldn't help but smile, his mood notching higher. His daughter might be racing toward lipstick and a driver's license, but at eight, Lee looked the same as he had at two. He still loved trucks and dinosaurs; and give him some sort of ball and he would amuse himself endlessly. So blissfully uncomplicated. So unlike—

"Daddy," his daughter said. "You messed up *again*."

Mick made a mental eye roll. "Yeah, how's that? Is my handwriting not good enough where I signed off on your homework? Or have we forgotten something at the store you need for school? It's my volunteer day, so I can bring it when—"

"No. You forgot to mark Kayla's birthday on the calendar. I remember the date and it's the Sunday after this one."

"Kayla's birthday?" He didn't know it off the top of his head, but every year when they got a new calendar he paged through the old one in order to mark down important events. It was something he recalled his mom doing, and as a single parent, he'd taken on the habit for himself. "I can't believe I missed that."

"It doesn't matter," the nanny said, as she pulled out a chair for Lee at the kitchen table.

"Birthdays matter," Jane countered.

"Not so much when you're turning twenty-seven."

Mick frowned at that. Twenty-seven. Last night, Austin had mentioned she was a woman, and of course Mick had been noticing she was a woman for six months now, but still…twenty-seven. She wasn't any kid. At twenty-seven he'd already been married and a father two times over.

"We have to have cake and presents," Lee said as he dug into the bowl of cold cereal Kayla had poured for him. "And balloons, and…"

Mick half listened to his son ramble on about his favorite birthday elements. He didn't think Kayla would want pony rides or an inflatable party jumper shaped like a pirate ship. Instead, he pictured her across a small table. A white cloth, wineglasses, gleaming knives and forks. A date scene. Definitely a date scene, because the menu he was envisioning with that table didn't include any kind of kid entrées.

"We'll go out," he said, cutting through Lee's Cheerios-muffled voice.

Kayla frowned at him. "I can get my own dates."

That's right. Although she didn't seem too excited about the one she'd set up with Betsy the night before. "I didn't mean—" he started.

"I'm sure I'll be doing something with my family anyway," she said, turning away. With quick steps, she crossed to the refrigerator and started removing the standard basics that comprised his kids' lunches.

He bent to retrieve the white-but-whole-wheat loaf from the bread drawer. For a few minutes their morning was like it always was when he wasn't at the station. The kids chattered, he and Kayla responded, even as they moved about the kitchen like a couple of contestants in that celebrity dancing show that Janie loved. In sync. He slapped the bread on the board, she spread the mayo, he squeezed the mustard. Turkey, a very thin slice of tomato (Janie was very particular about that), a crisp piece of iceberg.

When had they turned into a team?

No. He was merely being a father. She was just doing her job.

But that thought was so...unworthy, that he couldn't stop himself from saying, "If you're busy on your birthday, we can choose another day."

"The Thunderbird Diner," Jane put in. "Me and Lee love the fries there."

"I want onion rings," Lee corrected. "I had them when I went there with Jared and his parents."

Mick tried to ignore the small wrench of disappointment he felt at their words. Of course the kids would want to be included. Of course that was the appropriate way to celebrate their nanny's special day.

But he couldn't stop himself from seeing it in a

completely different manner. He could suffer through a tie. And she'd smell great, as a matter of fact like she smelled right now, a scent that was mostly flowery but with the slightest of spicy notes that said feminine with staying power. So Kayla.

He'd put his fingertips at the small of her back as they walked into the restaurant. The little twitch she made at his touch would mean that her breath had caught…and then his breath would catch, too. Once they were seated, their server would ask if it was a particular occasion like an anniversary or a birthday. Kayla would look at him, her heart in her eyes, because she would dislike any widespread attention. So he'd smile and just say it was always an occasion when he was out with a beautiful woman.

Then Kayla would—

"Daddy," his daughter whispered, breaking the bubble of his fantasy.

He shook himself and stared down at her. "What?"

Jane's face was so familiar…and yet so different. The cheekbones were sharper against her skin, her eyes seemed wider than ever before and her neck longer, somewhere between gangly and elegant. When she opened her mouth, that gap between her front teeth told him that he needed to make that orthodontist appointment he'd been putting off. A now-familiar sensation constricted his chest and he reached out to slide his hand down her hair.

"Daddy," she said again, under the conversation that Kayla and Lee were conducting about the merits of French fries versus onion rings. "We need to get Kayla the perfect gift."

He could see it. Other years it had been scarves and stationery and coffeemakers, but he knew her better now. He could see himself in that certain department he always made sure to keep his gaze averted from and there he would find something... not slinky, nothing so cheesy. Kayla's blond beauty would look best in a flowing garment, fragile layers that would only briefly cling to her curves and then float away.

Oh. Oh, man. It wasn't that he knew her better now; it was that he wanted to *know* her better now.

He shifted away from his daughter to pack the lunch items into Lee's lunchbox and Jane's brown sack—the last teen heartthrob lunchbox had been tossed away in a fit of preteen "maturity." Kayla joined him at the counter, completing her part of the morning ritual. Their hands both closed over the same sandwich bag of apple slices.

She raised her gaze to his.

It was his turn to twitch. Damn! How had this happened? He'd been no more aware of her than he'd been of the…the teakettle on the stove. But then he'd caught her almost kissing that bristle-haired Lothario and everything had changed.

He'd developed this weird overprotective thing. That was all. He'd realized that she was a woman, not just the nanny, and he'd felt responsible for her because she was a member of his household.

Yeah.

Her brows came together. "What's wrong?"

He'd claimed he could see inside of her, but clearly that went both ways—she knew he was unsettled. All because he saw her as a woman now, and because, damn it, he didn't want to see her as a woman! He had enough on his plate without taking on this…this…

"I'm fine," he said, turning so that he was no longer meeting her gaze. She was so pretty. And, face it, sexy.

The acknowledgment of that slid over him like a hot hand, stiffening his muscles, putting every cell of his body on hyperalert. She stood at his left side, just a few inches away, and his skin prickled, his pulse pounding against his flesh like a drumbeat.

His mind flashed on lingerie, intimate dinners, candlelight. He pivoted toward her. "Kayla…"

How could he ever have viewed her as a child or a girl or anything less than a full-grown, fully attractive woman? How could anyone miss that shiny golden hair and the vivid blue of her beautiful eyes? As he looked down at her he saw a rush of goose bumps scurry down her throat toward her breasts.

His mouth dried. He saw her tongue dart out to wet her top lip and in another mind-flash he wondered if she was wet somewhere else. Kayla. Wet for him. His body twitched again.

"Kayla," he repeated. Perhaps it was time to come clean. Perhaps it was time to tell her he was thinking of private meals, sheer fabrics, hot skin. He glanced up and could see on her face a combination of confusion and trepidation.

Still, he opened his mouth to tell her everything on his mind, but then that look on her face arrested him. Think, Hanson! *Confusion. Trepidation.*

Both were warnings that he should be cautious, too. What had he been thinking the other night as he sat beside Will? That he couldn't take on the responsibility of making another person happy.

Without a mother, Jane and Lee had to be his priority. Under the weight of making yet another relationship work he might crack, and then where would his beloved children be?

Kayla put her hand on his arm. He jolted back, but then steadied so he wouldn't look like such a wuss.

Still, he felt her fingertips as if they branded him. His groin grew heavy. Just at that!

"Mick. What's wrong?"

"I..." He felt an explanation stick in his throat. He couldn't seem to mouth an excuse, and yet he couldn't seem to make a claim, either. His claim on her.

Her fingers caressed his forearm. "You can tell me."

And he thought again that maybe he should. Maybe he'd tell her that she wasn't just an employee in his eyes. That somehow she'd found her way under his skin and that perhaps they deserved a special night to explore what might be.

A trilling sound broke the bond between them. She took her hand off his arm to dig for her phone in her pocket. Her brows came together as she glanced at the screen and then she held the phone to her ear.

He moved away to give her a bit of privacy for her call. As soon as it was over, though, he *would* come clean, he decided. Caution be damned.

Seconds later she afforded him—and Jane and Lee—a lopsided smile. "Confirmation of my double date with Betsy tonight," she said. "It should be fun."

Her date with a stranger. It made Mick's skin itch. Even though she wouldn't be alone with the guy, this other man was likely someone unencumbered by children, memories and a reluctance to take on a relationship. Mick inhaled a breath. "Good for you," he said.

And tried to mean it.

Chapter Three

One Friday each month, Jane and Lee's school, Oak Knoll Elementary, devoted the morning to track-and-field sports. There were the usual sprints, longer distance runs and broad jump, as well as other non-Olympic-type events such as a bean bag toss and Mick's brainchild, the Impossible Football Catch.

Parents guided the children from the event positions that were set up and run by yet other volunteers. Mick usually enjoyed these Friday mornings—he made sure he attended all that his work schedule allowed—but today he found himself squeezing the football and staring off into space instead of anticipating the next classroom of kids to come by his station.

His partner that morning was Patty Bright. He'd known the short redhead with the splash of cinnamon freckles across her face for years. Her husband, Eric, too, since their daughter and Mick's had attended preschool together. Patty and his wife, Ellen, had been good friends, and the couple often invited him and the kids to social occasions at their house. Kayla, too.

Across the field his eye caught on the nanny as she moved to the twenty-five-yard dash with Lee and his classmates. School volunteer was not part of her nanny job description, but she'd started putting in hours as a requirement for a childhood development course she was taking in college. She'd continued the gig on a regular basis. She bent down to retie Lee's shoelaces, and Mick's fingers tightened on the football as his gaze focused on her round, first-class curves.

"Quite a sight, huh?" Patty said.

Mick gave a guilty jump and shifted his gaze to the other woman's face. "What?"

"I was just commenting on how tall Lee has grown in the past few months."

Grunting in acknowledgment, Mick pulled the brim of his ball cap a little lower on his head. *Geez,*

Hanson, he admonished himself. *You have no business checking out the nanny during school hours.*

He had no business checking out the nanny *any* time. So what that her silky blond hair rippled in the breeze and the little chill in the air turned the tip of her nose pink and reddened her luscious mouth? She was off-limits to him, and he was determined to see her as a competent caregiver, not some sexy—

Realizing he was staring at her again, he wrenched his gaze away and scuffed his shoe in the dirt. He wouldn't let her distract him again. "So, Patty, Lee looks like he's growing to you? I was just thinking this morning that he was still my dinosaur-lovin', veggie-hatin', grubby little boy."

Patty smiled. "When I look at him I see that little guy, but I also see a lot of Ellen, too."

Ellen. Mick jerked his head toward his son and inspected him from cowlick to rubber soles. Ellen. Yeah, he could see it now, too, the same straight, dark hair, the wide grin, the masculine version of his wife's adorable snub nose. His chest constricted, a little squeeze to remind him of how short their time here could be.

A hand touched his arm. "I'm sorry, Mick. I didn't mean to bring up bad memories."

"Don't worry about it." He found a smile. "Memories of Ellen aren't bad at all. We had a good life

together." Remembering that he was all alone to raise
the fruits of that good life—Jane and Lee—was what
would get to him at times. How could he make sure
he did the right thing by them? Could he stand up
to the responsibility of ensuring their health and
happiness?

"About that 'veggie-hatin'' of Lee's," Patty put
in, apparently eager to move on to another subject.
"They have cookbooks devoted to recipes that show
you how to hide them in things that kids will eat."

"I've heard of it," he said. Maybe that was a present he could give Kayla for her birthday. Sort of like
the vacuum cleaner his dad had gifted his mom one
year. She'd locked him out of their bedroom for a
week following the incident, and that might not be a
bad thing in this case, either.

Not that he was anywhere near Kayla's bed.

But he'd thought of her there during the last six
months. Her room was a floor away from his and he
had no way of hearing her moving around inside it.
Despite that, he'd imagined her in that room with the
pale blue walls and white trim. Her bed linens were
white too, the comforter lacy, and he'd pictured her
tossing and turning between her sheets, just like he
so often did, while replaying a smile she'd shot him
over Janie's head or the accidental bump of her elbow
against his ribs as they prepared a meal.

Something as simple as that smile or touch would arouse him in the privacy of his bed. There. He'd admitted it. For six months, thoughts of Kayla had been amping up his sexual meter. Sure, he'd reexperienced the natural urge for sex once the worst of his shock and grief over Ellen's death had passed. But this feeling was different. It had an edge to it that got harder and harder—oh, jeez, that word worked—the more he smelled Kayla's skin and the more he watched her move.

Once again, he remembered that night he'd witnessed her kiss on the porch. Damn him! And damn her, too, because the moment she'd brushed past him to go inside, her shoulder glancing his chest, a soft strand of her hair grazing the back of his hand, everything inside of him had shifted. Altered.

But he was working to put that "everything" back to rights, wasn't he? She was the nanny, he was the daddy and that was all there was to it.

"Mick…" There was a new hesitance in Patty's voice.

He turned to her. "What?"

The woman bit her lip. "Well…"

Frowning, Mick tucked the football under his arm. "What's the matter?"

"It's about Kayla. Well, about you and Kayla."

Mick froze, hoping like hell she hadn't guessed

his secret. He kept his voice nonchalant. "What do you mean? There's no 'me and Kayla.'"

It was Patty's turn to frown. "Well, of course there is. She's your nanny."

"And I've never thought of her in any other way." Mick voiced the quick lie. Although he didn't think Patty expected he'd never have another woman in his life, he didn't want her speculating on this crazy little…interest he had in the woman caring for his children. He was putting it from his head, wasn't he?

The puzzled expression on Patty's face made Mick puzzled in turn. He cleared his throat. "I'm sorry, Pat, but what exactly are you getting at?"

She sighed. "You know it's an unspoken rule of parenthood that you don't poach on other couple's babysitters."

"Sure." When Ellen had been alive, they'd learned that lesson right away when they'd asked the family down the street for the names of some reliable sitters. Not everyone was willing to share, and you had to approach the subject with as much delicacy as prying open an oyster for the pearl inside.

"So I wouldn't just go to Kayla myself, not without checking with you first," Patty assured him.

Frowning, he studied his friend's freckled face. "What the heck are you dancing around?"

She took a quick breath, and then the words tumbled out. "Eric has been offered the chance to work in the London office this summer. Well, starting late spring actually. And I think we're going to move—all of us. Danielle and Jason, too."

Danielle and Jason, Patty and Eric's kids who were the same age as Jane and Lee. "Sounds like a great opportunity," Mick said.

"Even greater if sometimes Eric and I could take a few weekend jaunts around Europe, just the two of us," Patty added. "Though there'll be other times it would be all five."

"Five?" His brow furrowed, then he got it. "You... you would like to take my nanny with you for three months?"

Patty bit her lip again. "It could last up to a year if we like it," she confessed.

Mick didn't know what to say. This was poaching of the first order! Taking his K—his nanny—away from his kids. Out of the country!

His expression must have looked thunderous, because Patty grimaced. "I know, I know. But I just had to ask, Mick. My kids love Kayla and I would feel completely comfortable leaving them in her hands when Eric and I could get away to Edinburgh or Paris. And it would be an opportunity for Kayla, too.

She told me that she traveled in Europe one summer. It sounded like a fabulous time for her."

Better than the years she'd spent hanging around a grumpy old widower, he supposed.

"I was thinking she'd go with us to Hawaii this summer," he muttered. It wasn't the British Museum or the Louvre, but at their young age, Jane and Lee wouldn't really appreciate a trip like that.

Patty nodded. "My kids would rather we were going to learn to surf as well, but this is an opportunity that might not come our way again. The company will pay for a lot of it and I've never been anywhere east of Dallas, Texas."

He scuffed at the dirt with the toes of his running shoes, unsure what to say. Sure, it would be a great opportunity for everyone…everyone but him and Jane and Lee. "The kids wouldn't want to lose Kayla," he said, focusing on them.

"And you'd miss her, too, I know," Patty added.

He didn't dare look up. "So…"

"So I was also thinking that your kids are getting older, Mick. Before they get too attached to their nanny, I thought you might be considering making a…a change."

Change! There was that poisoned word again. Change was what had messed up his ordered life.

The change in how he saw Kayla made him edgy. Frustrated. Damn needy.

But maybe Patty had something there. To get back to sanity, perhaps another change *was* required. He closed his eyes for a moment, depressed by the damn thought, then he looked over at his friend. "Could you give me a little time? To broach the idea with the kids and with Kayla? But by next week...by next week I'll tell her about your offer, okay?"

Patty smiled. "Okay." Her expression turned hopeful. "Or sooner?"

"Sure." He ignored his tight chest and the urge to glance around and assure himself that Kayla was still, for now at least, in the vicinity. "Or sooner."

Mick had half promised sooner, and even considered telling Kayla that very day, but obstacles kept getting in the way. She took off on errands in the afternoon. Then Jane and Lee were home, and he didn't want to discuss the subject with them in the room.

As he and Kayla made dinner, the kids got their weekend homework out of the way at the kitchen table. It was like it always had been, the kids fairly diligent, he and the nanny supplying help when necessary. As usual, they bickered with good nature over the best way to remember the spelling of the words on Lee's test.

The only difference this evening was that he could hardly stop staring at Kayla's mouth or finding some excuse to brush against her. His skin felt shrink-wrapped to his bones and inside he burned like a three-alarm fire.

He had it bad, and depressing thought or no, Patty had provided a prescription for relief.

"Kayla," he said, keeping his voice low. "I'd appreciate it if we could have a talk after dinner. Just, uh, just the two of us."

She glanced up at him, her face coloring. "Just the two of us?"

He shifted, embarrassed at how intimate he'd made it sound. "I mean, I want to talk about the kids."

"Oh. Right. The kids." Her head bobbed up and down. "But…Mick, I'm sorry, I have to get ready now for my date. I won't be here for dinner…or after."

"Ah. Yeah. Sure. Some other time." He felt like an idiot, because he was holding plates in his hands, ready to set the table for four. He'd forgotten about Kayla and her date.

She hurried out of the kitchen while he just stood there, his mind replaying her words. *I won't be here for dinner…or after.* She'd be with some other man for dinner…and after.

It couldn't be jealousy, he told himself, but God, the taste of something bitter and green stuck to his tongue. He served up the plates for himself and the kids, hoping that the chicken and rice would dissipate the god-awful taste.

The food smelled good enough.

The scent of it lingered in the kitchen as they ate and even as he cleaned up the dishes. But then a new note entered the atmosphere, one that drew him around immediately.

Kayla's perfume. And oh, God, there she was, in a silky short black dress, her hair gleaming against her shoulders. Her lashes were darker than usual, her mouth a soft and tender pink, and she was holding toward him a necklace of delicate links and a pearl pendant. "I hate to ask, but could you help me with this? I can't get it latched."

He took it from her, feeling as if the tendons in his joints had tightened to short steel cords. Without a word, he signaled for her to turn around, and she did, then held her fall of hair off her neck.

Her beautiful neck, the skin looking so sweet and delectable. Tempting. In a flash of lust, he saw himself putting his mouth against the thin flesh at its side and pressing against it a hot, sucking kiss.

Good God, he groaned silently. Yeah, he had it bad. Really bad.

So bad that as he breathed in her scent and felt the heat of her just inches from his hard, tense body, his clamoring need had him wondering if there wasn't another prescription altogether he should be considering for his sexual relief.

Already nervous about the evening's date, Kayla nearly jumped out of her skin when Mick's fingers brushed her neck. A wash of goose bumps paraded from her nape southward and she hoped he wouldn't notice the reaction. This was silly, right? She was determined to overcome these teenagerish, twitchy nerves.

But his warmth at her back didn't make it any less difficult. It was just too easy to imagine leaning against his chest, turning her head to take a kiss....

"Kayla?"

She made that turn she'd been picturing, she even found herself staring at his mouth. Heat washed over her as another band of goose bumps marched down her skin.

"Kayla, I..." He hesitated, his palm coming up to cradle her jaw.

The goose bumps took another lap. "You can say anything," she whispered to him, not even sure what she meant by the words. "Anything."

"What's it like going out on a date?"

At Jane's loud question, she and Mick jolted back from each other, his callused hand trailing for just a moment along her skin.

The young girl surveyed Kayla, then sighed. "You look so pretty."

"Thank you," Kayla said, managing a smile.

"So what's it like going out on a date?" Jane asked again.

Mick stepped forward. "Remember our agreement, little girl. Not until you're thirty-one."

His daughter didn't even pretend to believe him. "Daddy, you're silly. I'm talking to Kayla. I want to know what happens on a date."

"Uh…" Kayla shot Mick a glance.

He lifted his hands. "Don't look at me. The last date I had was so long ago I think I was still in the fire academy."

She frowned at him. "I seem to remember a certain someone meeting a certain someone else at a coffeehouse a few months back." Though she'd kicked herself for it, she'd been relieved when he'd freely admitted there'd been zero chemistry between himself and the lady.

He shrugged it off.

"So…?" Jane prompted.

Kayla pushed her hair over her shoulders. "It's like…like sitting next to someone new in the school lunchroom. You get a chance to listen to them talk, hear what's important to them—"

"I always look at what they eat," Jane put in. "The ones with the good mothers cut their sandwiches in triangles."

Kayla's heart squeezed. While Jane didn't have a mother in her life any longer, Kayla did cut her sandwich into triangles...it was what she'd wished her mother had done when she was little. She smiled at Jane. "Like that, but remember I cut Lee's in half."

The girl rolled her eyes. "He thinks it makes him macho."

"Hey," Mick said. "I thought we weren't supposed to judge a book by its cover. Now we're deciding on the quality of people's parentage by the contents of their lunchbox and the shape of their PB and Js?"

His daughter ignored him again. "What do you talk about, though? I think I'd like to go to a movie on a first date so that it would do all the talking for us."

"When you're older the talking part gets a little easier," Kayla said. "You can ask a guy about his work, his family, if he has any pets. Some men like to talk about their car."

"Stay away from that kind," Mick said, grimacing. "Deadly dull. Only thing duller is if he wants to expound on his fantasy football team."

"Oh," Kayla groaned, closing her eyes for a moment. "Why do I feel like this is going to be a disaster?"

"We could come up with a signal," Mick offered. "You know, you call home to check on things and I'll claim we need you back immediately."

She groaned again. "You really think it's going to be that bad?"

His expression softened. "No. I'm sorry. I shouldn't be bringing up worst-case scenarios." He reached out a hand to brush the hair away from her forehead.

At the touch, she couldn't stop the little jerk of her body. He froze, his fingers still wrapped by strands of her hair, his eyes narrowing. His thumb drew a short stroke at her hairline and then another.

A shiver jittered across her scalp and then down her spine. She didn't even try to hide it from him. Mick let out a breath. "Kayla," he said softly.

The tenderness in his voice and the sudden raw tension in the air between them made Kayla's belly tighten. Desperate to break the invisible cord, she jerked her head around, looking for his daughter.

"Jane…" she said, her voice too breathless.

"Didn't you hear Lee's bellow?" Mick asked. "Their favorite TV show came on. She scampered out."

Meaning they had relative privacy in the kitchen,

and he was warm and strong and touching her still…
Another shiver jittered over her.

"Are you okay?" His fingers trailed over her hair
and then his arm dropped.

She shook her head, looking away from him. It
didn't help. He hadn't moved, meaning she could still
feel his body heat and the weight of his gaze. Both
scrambled her thinking and made her heart pound
too fast.

"Kayla." He curled his forefinger under her chin,
lifting her head so their eyes met. "What is it?"

She swallowed, then shrugged a shoulder in a nonchalant gesture. "I'm nervous, that's all."

His head cocked. "Of me?"

"No!" Of course it wasn't him. She made *herself*
nervous, anxious to ensure she didn't give away her
unwanted, unwarranted desire for this attractive,
sexy, *ineligible* man. "You know, it's that first date
thing."

He was still holding her chin, now pinched between his thumb and forefinger. "What specifically
is bothering you?"

She watched his mouth move as he said the words.
His lips looked soft, the slight edge of whiskers
around them only serving to outline their manly
shape. "It's…it's the kiss," she heard herself blurt.
"Maybe I've forgotten how."

Heat washed up her cheeks. Great. She really wasn't thinking about kissing some man she'd never met, of course. It was Mick who was making her say silly, senseless things. It was thinking of him, his mouth, his tongue, his taste that was rattling her brain and tripping up her pulse. With a little shuffle of her feet, she tried moving out of his grasp.

His grip tightened, just those two fingers making her immobile, keeping her captured as he bent close. "Then let me remind you," he whispered, his breath warm against her face, "of exactly how two pairs of lips are supposed to meet."

Chapter Four

Kayla let herself into the quiet house at the end of her date. It was barely eleven, but the family was obviously already upstairs for the night. It was past the kids' bedtime.

She clicked off the lamp left burning for her in the living room and crossed toward the kitchen. On the threshold, she hesitated.

Don't think about what happened in there, she instructed herself. *Put it straight from your mind.*

Her heels tip-tapped on the wooden floorboards. Just a few hours ago she'd been standing right beside the sink, her skin heating up beneath the cool chain Mick had just fastened around her neck and then—

Don't think about it!

In her bedroom, she quickly slipped off her dress. Her cell phone rang as she pulled her sleeveless, thigh-length nightshirt over her head. The fire alarm–styled ring tone signaled that her boss had dialed her number. She froze, instincts warring. On the one hand, a purely feminine impulse urged she ignore the call. On the other, the nanny in her itched to answer. Was something wrong with Jane or Lee? Had the evening included a domestic disaster she should know about?

Yet another thought galvanized her: *If you don't pick up, he might come downstairs. Right into this room!*

Her leap for the phone was worthy of the elementary school's track-and-field Friday. "Hello?" The sudden broad jump had made her breathless.

"Kayla." Mick sounded concerned. "Are you okay? Is something wrong?"

She swallowed, trying to calm her galloping heart with the palm of her free hand. His deep voice, however familiar, had flustered her. "I'm good. Fine. Is there something wrong with *you?*"

There was a long pause. He muttered something she didn't catch. "Mick?"

"No. Nothing's wrong," he said. "I wanted to warn you…"

Had the kids seen something? Asked him about the— *Don't think about that!*

He started again. "Now, don't be mad—"

"I'm not mad," she said. "Why would I be mad? I mean, what's there to be mad about?"

The silence on the other end of the line was puzzled. "Uh, I haven't gotten to the part you might be mad about yet."

"Oh." He wasn't talking about the...thing she shouldn't think about in the kitchen. She'd thought he thought she might be mad about that thing. Her hand massaged her forehead. "What *are* you talking about?"

"I wanted to warn you...and apologize. The kids and I built a metropolis in Lee's room and I didn't make them pick it up before bed."

"Oh." He'd been so unimpressed with the thing she didn't want to think about in the kitchen that he'd spent the evening—unlike her—not worrying about it, and instead building one of the extensive wooden blocks-and-LEGO worlds that used up acres of floor space and a ton of primary-colored toys. "That sounds like fun."

"But now we're all just one misplaced footstep away from agony. So, fair warning."

"Ah." Yes, more than once the bottom of her bare

soles had found the sharp edge of a plastic brick. Agony described it well. "I understand."

"The kids and I'll take care of the cleanup in the morning."

"Okay. Thanks." Good. Really good. With that little exchange it was as if the thing in the kitchen had not happened at all and they were back to their stable boss-employee relationship. Discussing toys, kids and cleanup. See, nothing had changed.

"Was your evening, uh, enjoyable?" Mick asked now.

She swallowed. "Sure. Betsy and I and our dates had dinner, then we saw a movie," she said, adding the name of the latest action-adventure blockbuster.

"Did you like it? I saw a trailer for it and the plot sounds kind of far-fetched."

It had a plot? She didn't remember the sequence of events or even the faces of the actors in the movie. Her mind had been on another reel altogether, and it had kept playing and replaying in her head, a loop of—

"Kayla?"

"It was pretty spectacular," she admitted.

"There were explosions?" Mick asked.

"I thought the top of my head might come off."

"Wow. That intense, huh?"

"Intense doesn't—" She stopped herself. He was

discussing the movie, she suddenly realized, while she...she was not. "I think you'll have to see it for yourself."

"I just might do that."

An awkward pause ensued. Kayla shivered a little, and pulled back the covers so she could get under the sheets and comforter. "Anything else to report?"

"Like what?"

She could wrap this up, she supposed. Say goodnight. But as she settled back against the pillows, she found herself reluctant to end the call. Maybe because it took her mind off places it shouldn't be wandering, she told herself. "I never asked you how your part of track-and-field day went. Impossible Football Catch another success? It's always popular."

"Because I dish out Life Savers candies on the sly. Don't tell."

"Mick Hanson!" She pretended to scold. "You know as well as I do there's a rule against providing sugary treats during the school day."

His voice lowered until it was almost like a whisper in her ear. "What'll I have to give you to keep my secret?"

Her secret made itself known then, as a rash of goose bumps broke out over her skin. He didn't have to do that thing she didn't want to think about. He didn't have to touch her in any way at all. The

forbidden attraction she had for him made itself
known anyway. "I…I…" She felt tongue-tied and
awkward and worried he'd suspect everything she
was trying to hide from just the squeaky tone in her
voice.

He saved her by clearing his. "So," he said, drop-
ping the subject of secrets. "Back to your date. Are
you planning on seeing this gentleman again?"

She couldn't even picture what the "gentleman"
looked like. His appearance had made that little of
an impression due to the fact that ninety percent of
her brain had been occupied with different visuals
altogether. Guilt gave her a little pinch. "He's very
nice."

Mick winced. "Ouch."

"What?" Guilt pinched her again because she
knew she'd barely given the nice guy the time of
day. "He represents a national window supplier and
he's successful, hardworking—"

"Transparent," Mick put in.

It took her a moment to catch on. "Hah. Window,
glass, transparent, I get the joke."

He laughed, low. "No flies on you, sweetheart."

At the endearment, her blood turned to honey in
her veins. The word itself moved, slow and sweet,
through her. Although goose bumps rose again on
her flesh, she had to kick off the covers. "Mick…"

"Hmm?"

But she didn't have anything to add. She'd only wanted his name on her tongue as her physical response to him overtook her once again. It wasn't good, she knew that. But being good had gone out the window just a few hours ago, when—

"Did my, uh, little reminder come in handy tonight?" Mick asked, his voice very, very soft.

And then it happened. What she'd been trying to prevent since she'd walked back into the house. The memory of Mick's little "reminder" burst in her head like a time-lapse photo of a blooming flower.

Both of his hands had moved to cup her face. The palms were a little work-roughened, and warmer, even, than the heat climbing up her neck and into her cheeks.

She'd flinched a little at the contact and he'd murmured to her, in the same tone she figured he'd use for a treed kitten. "Shh. Stay still now."

Her fingers had fisted at her sides instead of reaching out and hanging on to him like they'd wanted to. She'd watched his face descend until she was afraid this pre-moment kiss was just a dream. Then she'd closed them and felt her heart pounding harder against her breastbone. *Mick,* she'd thought to herself. *Mick is a breath away from kissing me.*

Of course he'd been gentle. At first.

At first it had been with sweet affection. Instead of relaxing, though, she'd tensed more at that tender touch, half-afraid that it was the sum total of the lesson he had for her—and half-afraid it wasn't. When he'd increased the pressure by just the smallest amount, she'd parted her mouth. The tip of his tongue had met the silky underside of her bottom lip. Icy heat had washed over her skin and she'd grabbed his waist before her knees failed her.

He'd moved into her hold. Into her mouth.

Their tongues had tangled. She'd smelled his soap, felt his heat radiating toward her, tasted him.

Wanted more.

Wanted him.

Her nipples had contracted in an almost-painful rush as her mouth widened to take his deeper thrust. His hands had moved, one sliding around to the back of her head, the other sliding over her shoulder and down her spine. She'd felt his palm bump over the strap of her bra and her breasts had swelled, aching for him to touch her there, too.

"Kayla," he'd said against her lips. She'd felt his hold loosen, his kiss gentle. As reluctant as she'd been to let him go, she'd forced her hands to drop away from him.

"Kayla," he said again now.

"Yeah, Mick?" she managed.

"I don't regret it," he admitted, obviously reading her mind.

She did. She'd been right not to want to think about what had happened between them in the kitchen. Because when she did, she was very afraid no other man, no other kiss, would ever measure up.

The following Saturday, Mick woke to the light bounce of his mattress and a click from the television situated in the walnut-finished armoire across from the bed. Soon it was emitting zany, cartoon noises. Then came another, weightier bounce followed by the meow of a cat. He opened his eyes just as the animal settled on the small of his back.

His gaze landed on his children, their eyes glued to the TV set. Lee was in the middle, his hair in its characteristic cowlick of surprise. His daughter, à propos of who she was at eleven, clutched a gossip-and-fashion magazine aimed at preteen girls, although her attention was captured by the television screen.

Mick sighed as the cat started purring against his spine and Lee's kneecap dug a friendly hole in his rib cage. Not only didn't he have metaphorical room for a woman in his life, there was literally zero space for her in his bed. Really, it was as simple as that.

"Dad," Lee said, his eyeballs tracking the movement on the TV.

"Yeah?"

"You think La-La will make me my favorite Saturday breakfast this morning?"

And there you go. The opposite of simple. Not just because of that, uh, lesson in the kitchen the week before, but because of that still-unspoken European offer on the table. Both had rolled through his mind, oh, about a thousand times in the last eight days. He'd still not mentioned Patty's proposition to the nanny, though.

"I can make your favorite breakfast, pal," he told Lee. "We shouldn't rely on Kayla for everything, you know. What, um, *is* your favorite Saturday breakfast?"

"I decided last weekend when you had to work," his son said, over Jane's mock retching noises. "Open-faced grilled cheese."

"That's not so bad."

"With pickle relish on top."

Mick felt a little like retching himself and he stirred, disturbing the cat so that it leaped off the bed with a disgruntled *"lurp."* "I can do that. *We* can do that, the three of us together."

After he dressed in workout gear, they paraded down to the kitchen to prepare breakfast then, and over the relish fumes Mick thought it was perhaps time to bring up the subject of the nanny and her future with their family. He didn't want to go into much detail—he'd save that until he heard Kayla's own reaction to the offer—but it made sense to remind his children that she wasn't a permanent fixture in the household.

"You know, guys," he began. "Kayla—"

"Kayla what?" Her voice asked.

He started, jerking around to see her stepping through the doorway that led to the short hall and her private quarters, dressed in her long flannel robe and slippers. "I...I..." Something had to be said, yes? Though he realized he was just staring at her, remembering the scent of her perfume, the smooth skin of her nape as his fingertips brushed it when he latched the necklace, the soft press of her lips as she kissed him back.

She'd kissed him back. God, hadn't that felt great?

The hem of her robe fluttered around her ankles as she made for the coffee. He dropped his eyes to stare at her bare ankles instead of her mouth, but he'd already noted the tired look in her eyes. Maybe she'd been experiencing fitful nights of sleep, too.

"You look tired," Jane commented, turning in her chair. "Were you dreaming about your date from last week? You never said how handsome he was. And what about sexy?"

"Sexy!" Mick frowned at his daughter. "That's not appropriate kind of talk." Then he slid his gaze toward the nanny, trying to assess her unspoken response for himself.

Yeah, how sexy was he?

Kayla's cheeks were pink. "Your father's right, Jane. You shouldn't ask other people about—"

"But is he The One?"

"And not that, either," Kayla scolded. She poured herself a cup of coffee and then topped off Mick's. "Lee conned you into grilled cheese and relish?"

"I've decided I could market this concoction as a diet aid. The smell of it at 8:00 a.m. has put me right off my own breakfast."

Her gaze lingered on his chest, then cut away. "I think you're right. I'll shower before I eat anything. You have it handled in here?"

"Of course." It hit him, then, that she was standing exactly where she'd been last week when she'd complained about forgetting how to kiss.

As if she remembered as well, her gaze lifted to his. Their eyes locked like their lips had done. There was something besides the scent of coffee and pickle relish in the air. The atmosphere crackled with a tension that edged down Mick's back like the sensuous scratch of a woman's fingernails.

"I should go…." Kayla murmured.

"Don't," he heard himself say. He didn't want her to go. Not away from the kitchen. Not away from him.

Then Lee bounced between the two of them, breaking the bubble that had seemed to enclose the pair of adults. Mick moved back to give his son more space and remembered again.

He didn't have room in his life for anyone. Even for Kayla.

She disappeared in the direction of her room, closing the hall door behind her. Mick let out a long breath of air and turned back to the breakfast prep. "We've got to get a move on. Two basketball games this morning." Both his children played in the local rec league and he coached the teams himself.

"Daddy," Jane said, "can I go home with Kayla between the time mine ends and Lee's begins? I'll be b-o-o-o-red with nothing to do but sit in the bleachers."

"I don't know that she'll be coming to basketball today," he replied.

Lee turned to stare at Mick as if he'd spilled there was no Santa Claus. "But La-La comes to watch everything I do."

Oh, boy. Due to his firefighter's schedule, their nanny didn't have the regular eight-to-five, Monday-through-Friday gig that she might have with another family. It meant she did chauffeur the kids to—and attend—events that would normally be a parent's responsibility.

"Lee, I'm off today. That means Kayla can do whatever she wants. Maybe she'd rather go shopping or read a book or see a movie."

His son merely blinked. "La-La comes to watch everything I do," he repeated.

Like a mother, Mick thought, feeling his belly clench. He reached out and wrapped his big hand around Lee's neck to draw him in for a hug. "I know, pal, and you've been lucky in that. But we have to respect her days off."

"Remember how she came back early from that girls' weekend she went on to see my ballet recital?" Jane pointed out.

"She *likes* to watch me play, Dad." Lee pulled away and headed toward the door leading to the nanny's room. "We can ask her—"

"No." Mick lunged for his son and caught him by the flannel pajama sleeve. "If you ask her, you'll put her on the spot."

Lee shot a glance at his sister. "Like when Jane asked her if her date was 'The One'?"

"Yeah. Like that." Although Mick couldn't help but remember that Kayla hadn't answered the question. "We should—"

"It was a stupid question," Lee proclaimed. "There's no The One for La-La. Not yet."

Jane brought over her empty cereal bowl to rinse in the sink. "How come? Are you still planning to marry her yourself when you grow up?" she teased.

Lee shoved his sister in the arm. "Shut up about that. I was just a baby when I said it."

"You said it like last week."

"Did not."

"Did, too."

"Did not."

"Wait, wait, wait." Mick laid a hand on the shoulder of each kid. "That's enough."

He had one of those parental headaches starting to throb at the base of his brain—yet another reason he couldn't bring a female into his life. How could you subject your children's Saturday morning bickering on another adult and look yourself in the eye? "You kids go up and make your beds and then get ready for basketball."

Lee's lower lip stuck out. "I only meant that La-La can't leave us until after I sign with the San Francisco Giants," he said. "You know, when I go pro."

The throb of Mick's headache kicked into higher gear. "Lee. Son."

"What?"

"Look. You need to understand…" He hesitated.

"Understand what?" Lee demanded.

"You see…" Mick couldn't get the words out.

Rolling her eyes, Jane jumped into the conversation. "He doesn't know how to tell you you'll never play professional baseball, brat-face."

"Jane." Mick shook his head. "Don't." Then he sighed. "Let's go sit down."

His feet were slow following the children to the kitchen table. How hadn't he seen this coming? He'd never thought about explaining to his kids that Kayla wasn't a permanent fixture in their family. At first he'd been too busy grieving, then too involved with keeping up, then…just so damn grateful that he'd probably taken it as much for granted as the eight- and eleven-year-old who expected her to make every basketball game and every ballet recital.

Damn! Some days single fatherhood especially sucked.

And he still didn't feel he should get into specifics about Patty and Eric Bright's Europe proposal until he found the right time and place to discuss it with Kayla. He'd run into a burning building with more eagerness than he felt at diving into this discussion with his kids.

Their expressions were apprehensive, he saw, as they settled around the table. Damn, he thought again. "Look, guys, there isn't anything to be worried about."

Except that the woman who's looked after you as long as you likely can remember may be leaving us for another family.

"Remember, we've talked about this kind of stuff before. Uh, life goes on. Winter, spring, summer, fall."

Lee nodded, ticking off on his fingers. "Basketball, baseball, swimming, soccer."

Mick grimaced. Leave it to his son to think of everything in terms of sports. "Well, that's right. We move on season to season. It would get pretty, uh, boring if we stuck with just basketball year-round."

Their expressions turned puzzled. "We play *H-O-R-S-E* even in the summer," Jane reminded him.

He tried again. "You know what I mean. Nothing lasts forever. You grow out of your favorite shoes. You stop obsessing over those little furry gizmos and take up yo-yos instead. You think you won't like your new teacher as much as the old one, but the new one turns out to be perfectly nice, as well."

Lee blinked. "I'm getting a new teacher?"

"No, brat-face," Jane said, comprehension appearing to dawn. "He's trying to tell you he ran over your bicycle."

His son gasped. "Dad!"

"I did not run over your bicycle, Lee." He shot a look at his daughter. "Not helping."

She flounced in her seat. "I don't understand what you're saying. I thought it was the bike."

"It's not the bike. It's not about toys or…teachers. Not exactly. I'm just trying to make sure you kids know that things change." And God, he hated that word, but pretending it didn't exist hadn't worked at all.

"Change how?" Jane asked, wary now.

He waved a hand. "Specifics aren't necessary. Not at the moment. But sometimes people find out that they've outgrown their current situation, like the shoes, you know? So you have to get a different pair and they're good, maybe even better than the old pair, which were getting a little ragged anyway."

"My last pair had that broken shoelace, remember?" Lee said. "La-La replaced it with a bright green one and they were as good as before. I didn't need any new ones until right before Christmas."

Mick stifled his sigh. He wasn't making himself

clear to his son. "But you eventually needed a new pair, didn't you?"

"Yes." Lee brightened. "Do you mean you think we should get Kayla new slippers for her birthday tomorrow? I saw you looking at the ones she was wearing earlier."

When he was avoiding looking at her mouth, he thought, focusing on the tabletop. "What I mean is that maybe we should be thinking about getting a new *Kayla*, kids."

A sound caught his attention. His head shot up, just in time to see their current Kayla disappear toward her bedroom. Oh, God. Had she heard him? And if she had...

Sighing, Mick dropped his head into his hand. Upon waking, he'd called his situation simple. What a crock, huh? It didn't take a genius to realize his circumstances were a thousand times more complicated than a too-small bed and a too-burdened heart.

Chapter Five

Following the morning basketball games, Kayla had a date for lunch with her friends from the nanny agency. Wearing a clingy knit dress in powder-blue and her black boots, she pushed open the glass doors of the large restaurant anchoring one corner of the mall. Her gaze immediately found the small cluster of women in the waiting area, each wearing a smile and carrying a brightly colored gift bag.

"Happy Birthday!" they chorused together.

She smiled at them, then was immediately swept along with the group as they followed the hostess to their table. Betsy linked arms with her. "Excuse me for saying so," she murmured, "but your celebration face seems a little sad around the edges."

"Of course not," Kayla started, then sighed. "Okay, maybe so. I guess it's the birthday blues." Or what she'd thought she'd overheard Mick say that morning. *We should be thinking about getting a new Kayla.* Had she misheard, or had he really expressed the sentiment?

Betsy directed Kayla to sit at the head of the table the hostess indicated. "I declare this a blues-free zone. We have presents! We're going to order desserts after lunch!"

Kayla relaxed against the back of her chair. "I'm being silly. Twenty-seven tomorrow isn't so bad."

"If you like, over lunch we can be seventeen instead," the irrepressible Betsy said.

"Good idea," agreed Jamie, another of the nannies. She had boy-short hair and took care of an "oops" infant whose closest sibling attended high school. "We'll talk about nothing but clothes, boys and sex."

"Shh!" Gwen, the head of the nanny agency, glanced around them even as she laughed. "We have a reputation to uphold, ladies."

Betsy leaned across the table. "Gwen. I'll have you know that nannies can have—" she paused and lowered her voice "—S-E-X, too."

Gwen raised an eyebrow. "I thought we'd all been unanimous in recently lamenting the deplorable state of our love lives."

Betsy grimaced. "Point taken. We'll leave it that nannies *want S-E-X,* too."

Their server arrived, derailing the discussion for the ordering of beverages and then their meals. As it was a birthday celebration, the friends agreed they should supplement their main course salads with an order of potato skins.

Jamie sighed as she swallowed a bite of the decadent appetizer. "Speaking of love lives, how did your double date go, girls?" Her gaze moved between Betsy and Kayla as they each remained silent. "That good, huh?"

"No sparks," Betsy admitted. Her glance cut over. "Kayla, you feel the heat?"

Not with the blind date. With Mick, before, during and after. She shook her head. "Mine called a couple of times since, but I've made excuses."

Betsy frowned, then brightened. "I may have another prospect. This very great-looking man moved into the house next door. He was a little put-out when my twin charges found their way into his backyard, but…did I mention he's great-looking?"

Given that Betsy was nanny to a pair of adorable but demonic four-year-olds, Kayla couldn't exactly fault the next-door neighbor's irritation, but she wasn't ready for another setup. "Why aren't you interested in him for yourself?"

Her friend was already shaking her head. "He grills meat. Every night, great hunks of meat."

Betsy was vegan—at least that was this month's claim. "I appreciate the thought, but I've decided to try finding my own men from now on," Kayla said.

So they spent the rest of the meal scoping likely prospects while eating lunch and giggling as if they were, indeed, seventeen again. The presents added to the festive atmosphere, and Kayla loved the matching scarf and gloves, the perfume, the books and candy she received from her friends. A dose of chocolate in the form of a triple-threat dessert only bubbled her mood higher.

It didn't crash until they were leaving the restaurant. "What's up for tomorrow?" Gwen asked. "Will the birthday girl be visiting with her parents?"

Kayla didn't let her smile fall, though. "Something like that." Nothing like that.

"And tonight?" Betsy queried. "Any plans?"

"I'm having dinner with an old friend from high school." Karen lived in Tucson now, but she had business in northern California. "It should be fun."

Betsy leaned in close. "Funner would be a man and *S-E-X*."

Kayla figured that possibility was as likely as contact with her parents on the actual day she turned another year older. But she kept her expression set on bright as she waved her friends goodbye and turned into the mall. Maybe she'd buy something new to wear.

She found herself on the children's floor at the department store, however, instead of at her favorite boutique. Lee needed new socks, she told herself. Lee always needed new socks. Turning down an aisle, she bumped into a familiar figure inspecting a rack of small shirts.

Betsy gasped in surprise, then looked sheepish. "You, too?"

"I'm after socks," Kayla said, then sighed. "Is there something wrong with us?"

"That we're spending a free Saturday shopping for our charges instead of for ourselves?"

"I just wonder what it says about me that I'd rather look at kids' clothing than a new pair of jeans."

Betsy ran her hands over her hips. "If you're me, it's because you've promised yourself to drop five pounds before buying another pair of pants."

Kayla didn't think that was why Betsy was really perusing blue clothes in size 4T. "A lot of people like their work, but I'm pretty sure it's not hip for women our age to be as into kids as we are."

The other woman toyed with a small button-down printed with a wild pattern of red biplanes. "When did you first start watching little ones?"

Kayla thought back. "I was twelve. The couple three doors down had an infant and an active social life. I was their go-to sitter until I started college. I took care of Lisa from when she was three months old. The first time I sat for both her and her little brother Curtis, he was only twelve days old. I was with them two to three times a week, even if only so their mom could meet a friend for a game of tennis or a cup of coffee."

"And you liked it."

She had. By then, her mother and father were both already remarried, each heavily involved in their new lives, and she'd showered on the kids she'd babysat the attention that she'd wanted for herself. The kids had given back to her as much as she'd given them, she'd realized early on. They were thrilled when she came to the house and sad when she went home.

Betsy nodded. "I was the neighborhood sitter, too. I've always wanted my own children."

"You don't worry that Duncan and Cal aren't filling up that place in your heart?"

"No." She grinned. "And if I were honest, there come some days when I thank God those little imps aren't mine 24/7. But then, Jana, their mother, admits they could try the patience of several saints."

Kayla knew her friend was devoted to the twins, but wondered if it was different for herself, the live-in nanny for motherless children. They didn't have a feminine presence besides herself who peeked in on them at night, no other woman pressed her palm to their foreheads checking for fever, not another female voice was in the house to calm their fears. Perhaps it was Mick's job that made her own different from Betsy's, too. With his twenty-four-hour shifts, there were times when she had all the responsibilities of a parent.

We should be thinking about getting a new Kayla.

What had that meant? She should have stopped in her tracks and demanded the answer. Instead, she'd let it stew into a bad-tempered brew that was now ruining her Saturday.

"You know, my oldest sister doesn't want kids, and I think that's fine," Betsy continued. "My cousin can't have any and she's made peace with that, too. Their feelings are legitimate and so are ours. There's nothing wrong with loving children."

But there was something wrong with Kayla's day and she was determined, she decided, to address it. "I've got to be going," she told her friend. No more letting it fester. She would confront Mick and find out just what was going on at the house on Surrey Street.

Minutes later she was pulling into the driveway. Gazing on the cream-and-green split level, she took a moment to gather her thoughts then strode to the front door. She reached for the knob just as Mick yanked it open. Her balance off, she swayed until he caught her by the shoulder.

Their eyes met.

The mood she'd brought back with her from the mall receded. His hand felt heavy, masculine, where it grasped her shoulder and heat zinged down her arm. He had gone without shaving that morning and the dark edge of whiskers only drew her attention to the shape of lips. Only helped her recall their tenderness on hers. Her mouth tingled now and she remembered that sizzling moment when his tongue touched hers and her heart had stopped.

His fingers gentled on her shoulder, the contact turning to a caress. She watched his chest expand on a breath. She, on the other hand, couldn't draw air into her lungs.

"Hey…" His voice was husky.

She remembered it speaking other words. *We should be thinking about getting a new Kayla.*

The memory galvanized her again. She jerked

away from him, and his arm dropped to his side. Narrowing her eyes, she focused on her goal. She had to get this out so she could clear the air and banish her blues. "Look," she said. "Pity parties are not my style, so—"

"So come along with me," he said, smiling.

It was the smile that undid her. "What?" But he had a hold of her again.

"We heard you drive up. The kids have been waiting all afternoon," he said, drawing her toward the dining room.

"Surprise!" yelled Jane and Lee.

Helium balloons bounced on the ends of ribbons attached to the backs of chairs. Presents sat on the long table, surrounding a cake with her name on it. The kids wore silly party hats and Lee started honking one of those loud party blowers. Kayla looked at Mick, then at the kids, then back to Mick again.

He shrugged. "We got a little excited and couldn't wait until tomorrow for your birthday."

Lee and Jane ran over. "You don't mind?" the girl asked.

Lee hugged Kayla so tight that her lungs felt like toothpaste in the tube. She was afraid they might be squeezed from her mouth, so she kept it shut and shook her head, blinking against the sting in her eyes. Her palms—those surfaces that had felt for fevers so many times—smoothed Lee's cowlick and the warm crown of Jane's head.

Stewing was done. Her mood hovered somewhere above those multicolored balloons. *There's nothing wrong with loving children,* Betsy had said.

There might be nothing wrong, but there might be something dangerous about loving two specific children who didn't really belong to her. Yet with them this close to her swelling heart, she didn't care.

The second hard-and-fast rule of nannydom had been broken eons ago, she realized, probably on some not particularly eventful night when she'd tiptoed in to turn off a light or tuck a stuffed animal beside a small, slumbering body.

She thought of Mick's children as hers, and no questions or clearing of air were going to change that.

Mick had been waiting all day to explain the comment he suspected the nanny had overheard that morning.

But watching her *ooh*ing and *aah*ing over her birthday gifts, he knew that replacing her would be impossible, just as it was impossible to look away from her now. The blue dress she wore accented her eyes and molded her slender body. High-heeled black boots made her legs go on forever.

Still, it wasn't his choice as to whether she would remain with them as the family nanny. He'd already stalled for more than a week without telling her about Patty's offer. And didn't he just feel low as a worm about that?

"Dad," Jane said, interrupting his thoughts. "Can we cut the cake now?"

"Sure, but you and Lee go hunt down the paper plates and the plastic forks, will you? A party shouldn't include doing dishes, not for any of us."

The kids scampered off, leaving him alone with Kayla in the dining room. She smiled at him. "I particularly like the loaded iPod. After I ruined mine in that unfortunate pool incident, I haven't replaced it because I couldn't bear the idea of having to take the time to re-create my playlists. Thanks for doing that, Mick."

"I'm ancient compared to you," he warned. "I know what you like to listen to, but I snuck some stuff on there you might consider oldies."

"Why do you keep bringing up our age difference?"

So I don't have to bring up the European proposal. So I can remember yet another reason why I shouldn't kiss you again. Sighing, he pulled out a chair to join her at the table. The sugary smell of the

frosting made his belly hurt—or at least he thought
it was that.

"Kayla—"

"We found 'em!" Lee bounded back in the room,
paper plates and plastic forks in hand. "Me wants
cake."

His gaze and Kayla's met across the table and they
both grinned. That was Lee's signature party line.
"He'll be saying 'me wants cake' on his wedding
day," Mick told her.

God. The thought of Lee marrying sobered him.
The boy was already eight and if these first years
were any indication, the next eight and the eight after
that would pass in the blink of an eye. His daughter
would marry, too—despite his avowed moratorium
on her dating. So where would that leave Mick? Who
would be at his side to watch his children move on
with their lives?

A profound loneliness leaked like dark ink into
his heart, making it throb instead of beat. He glanced
toward the living room and found the close-up photograph of his wife, Ellen, on the mantel. It was terrible
to admit, but he could hardly conjure up the sound
of her voice anymore. He didn't remember her scent.
But at times like this he missed her presence with an
ache sharp enough to cut.

"Mick."

He blinked, his gaze shifting to Kayla. At the other end of the table, the kids were forking down birthday cake like they hadn't been fed breakfast, lunch or dinner in a lifetime. Kayla pushed toward him his own serving on a paper plate decorated with more birthday balloons.

"I had a bit of the blues today myself," she said softly. "Is it catching?"

"Of course not, it's—"

"I know that look," she continued. "Where do you go, then?"

He realized she *would* know that look. Just as she knew when Jane required jollying or Lee needed to be headed off before turning into a whirling boy dervish, Kayla could read his moods.

Shaking his head, he frowned at her. "Who recognizes and tends to your bad moments?"

She waved a hand. Smiled. "Me? I don't have bad moments."

"You just said you did. Everybody does."

Jane piped up, making it clear she was getting to that age where she was acutely tuned to adult conversation. "Kayla talks to her nanny friends."

"You should be able to talk to us, too," Mick said. "Me."

"Or me," Jane added again. "You know, when you want to talk about boys and stuff."

Lee made a sour-lemon face. "Don't talk to me about boys. That makes me want to barf."

"But *I'd* like to hear it," Jane said. "I want to hear all about you finding The One."

Kayla laughed. "I don't know about this The One, Jane."

Mick's daughter turned to him. "Tell her, Daddy. Tell her The One is out there waiting." Then she didn't give him a chance. "My dad told us he saw my mom at a friend's wedding—she was a bridesmaid—and he said to himself, 'Well, hah. There she is.'"

"But she didn't like him right away," Lee put in, drawn into the story despite his professed repulsion to all things romantic. "She told him he was stuck-up and she didn't date good-looking guys."

Jane frowned. "Why did Mom say that? Why didn't she want to date cute boys?"

Mick shrugged.

"Because cute boys often know they're cute," Kayla said. "If they're courteous and cute, okay, but overconfident and cute...you have to be careful."

"I better say please and thank-you a lot, then," Mick said.

"Is that what made Mom change her mind about you?" Lee asked. "You remembered the golden rule and junk?"

Mick nodded. "And I remembered to wash my

hands when I was supposed to." Part of parenting was sneaking in a practical lesson at every opportunity.

Lee rolled his eyes.

Part of parenting was realizing your attempts to sneak in a practical lesson at every opportunity was extremely obvious, even to an eight-year-old.

"So Mom gave Dad a second chance to impress her," Jane said. "Maybe you need to give somebody a second chance, too, Kayla. You told me that man you went out with last week didn't wow you. Maybe *wow* doesn't happen on a first date."

Now it was Kayla's turn to shrug. "Or *wow* might be overrated. What about *hmm* or *maybe* or—"

"It should be *wow*," Mick said, firm on that.

She glanced over at him.

Mick's gaze tangled with hers. He was aware of the kids dashing off, likely fueled on sugary icing for the next week, but still he didn't say anything.

She broke the silence first. "So it was like that with you and your wife? Wow?"

"Yeah."

"Just like that," she persisted. "One look and wham. Bam. Wow."

"Yeah. But I was also in a place and time to be whammed, bammed and wowed," he said. "Not to mention I've always been a sucker for weddings."

Her expression was doubtful…or disappointed, he wasn't sure.

"I don't think *wow* has to hit like a frying pan, though," he added. "Maybe one day you wake up and look at someone you've known for a while and realize that the *wow* is right there in the room with you both."

And as he looked at her, he knew it was true now. *Wow* was as real as the balloons and the remainder of the birthday cake that read THDAY KAYLA. But for God's sake, he couldn't let *wow* lead him around this time! It might be zinging from wall to wall and floor to ceiling, but he was an older man, a widower, a father with two kids who couldn't just follow where *wow* led.

He had responsibilities; she had the world ahead to explore.

But he couldn't just blurt out the Europe offer to her now, either. Not with wrapping paper all around and balloons in the air. Not while she was putting in her earbuds and smiling at him like a hero for piecing together a playlist for her.

Goddamn, she was so sweet.

So hot.

And he wasn't ready to open the door for her to go away quite yet.

Chapter Six

Though it was technically her day off, Kayla pitched in with the cake cleanup and then the organization of the kids' evening events. Both had sleepover invitations that night and she would see them off before meeting her old friend for dinner. She handed the sleeping bags to Mick after fetching them from the hall closet.

"You have plans tonight, right?" he asked. "More birthday celebrating?"

"Sure."

"Your family?"

"Sure," she said again, though she didn't know why she bothered to lie about it. Still, it made her feel better, somehow, for Mick to think she was connected to something bigger, something like he had with his kids. She didn't want to feel like the unwanted, forgotten appendage to her mother's and father's new tribes, let alone have someone else—Mick—see her that way.

Jane showed up in the doorway to her room. "Help me find something to wear and then help me with my hair...pleaaase," she said, in that new dramatic manner she had, as if world peace and global hunger both dangled in the balance. "If you flat iron mine, I'll do yours."

Mick frowned. "Doesn't that flat-iron thing take a while? Kayla probably wants to relax before her big family deal tonight."

The big family deal that wasn't. Kayla could use a distraction from that fact. "Choosing clothes and playing with hair...there's nothing more relaxing than those two pastimes."

It didn't take long to pick out an outfit for Jane's sleepover. Mick was adamant that an eleven-year-old should dress like a girl and—as he'd said for Kayla's ears only—not like a sex-starved single woman. Because Kayla figured she *was* a sex-starved single woman, she had little trouble directing Jane to appropriate choices during shopping trips. Tonight they selected from the girl's closet a pair of lace-edged leggings and a two-piece tunic. A long, racer-back striped tee was layered over a white, peasant-styled blouse. With the addition of black flats, she looked appropriate *and* stylish.

They left the hall door leading to the bathroom open as they waited for the flat iron to heat. Jane's hair was as dark as her father's and thicker than Kayla's. The straightening process wasn't a quick one, but the shiny result was enough to make the effort worthwhile. Once they'd achieved the girl's straight, silky fall, Kayla switched places with her.

As Jane worked on a section of Kayla's hair, Lee wandered in to sit on the edge of the tub. "I like your hair the normal way, La-La. The wavy way, like a lasagna noodle."

Jane rolled her eyes. "Just what a woman wants to hear—being compared to something you serve with pasta sauce and cheese. You'll never get a girlfriend, Lee."

"Fine with me." He shrugged. "I don't want a girlfriend, not ever."

His sister shook her head. "You say that now. But what about when you're older? When you're in your twenties, do you want to be all alone?"

"La-La's in her twenties. She's all alone."

"Gee, thanks for that little reminder, buddy," Kayla said, grimacing. "But I should point out, Jane, that a person doesn't necessarily need a girlfriend or a boyfriend—a love interest, let's just say—in order to live a happy and complete life."

"Yeah, Jane," Lee chimed in. "Look at Dad. He doesn't have somebody and he's happy."

Jane pursed her lips and met Kayla's eyes. "Do you think that's so?" she asked softly. "Do you think he's happy?"

"I..." Kayla hesitated, unsure what to say. While it would be easy to tell Mick's daughter to put that question to the man herself, Jane was smart enough to know he'd answer in the affirmative no matter what the state of his true feelings. As the nanny, the caretaker of the children, wasn't it up to her to also float the possibility that Mick might find companionship one day? That it was a normal, healthy urge to want to share your life with another person?

"I think your father has you two special somebodies to love who keep his life very full," she finally replied, chickening out.

"My friend Drea's dad went on vacation to some beachy place and came home married to a woman she'd never met before—and that her dad had never met before his vacation, either! That would be so weird."

"Love can make people impulsive sometimes," Kayla said.

"What's *impulsive?*" Lee asked.

"When a person does something quickly and without a lot of thinking about it first."

"That doesn't sound like Dad," Lee announced, with an air of decided satisfaction.

It doesn't sound like me either, Kayla thought, though she wasn't certain she felt as content as Lee at the idea. Twenty-seven years old tomorrow, and she couldn't think of one time when she hadn't considered long and hard before doing anything more complicated than changing brands of toothpaste.

That Drea's dad had gone off on a vacation and come home with someone to love…well, right now that impetuous act sounded more romantic than wrong. She sighed to herself, wondering if that was what she needed—a change of scenery.

Or at least a drink with a little umbrella in it.

When she was out with Karen tonight, Kayla would order one with a silly-sounding name and see if her luck changed. She smiled at the thought and pleasant anticipation of the evening ahead blossomed.

"Still," Jane said, moving to work on the other side of Kayla's hair, "you never know. Dad could marry someone else, Lee."

The boy frowned. "Why would he want to do that?"

"To have a wife again. To get you a mother who will spank you when you're bad."

"Jane!" Kayla glared up at the girl. "Don't talk like that to your brother."

A glint appeared in the girl's eye. "Maybe she won't spank you, Lee. Maybe your new mother will only make you go to bed without dinner or video games."

"She'd be your mother, too—and maybe she'd say you're ugly and you smell like a pickle burp."

A pickle burp? Kayla just managed to hang on to her straight face. "*I'm* going to punish both of you with no TV tomorrow if you keep this up. Let's try to be nice to each other, huh?"

There was a common moment of semisullen silence, then Lee began thumping the heels of his rubber-soled shoes against the tub's porcelain. "I don't like talking about a new mother," he confessed. "I barely remember my real mother."

"Oh, Lee." Kayla's heart squeezed. He'd been only two when she'd died, so of course his memories had to be very dim, indeed.

"She used to have me pick out my barrettes before she brushed my hair in the morning," Jane said. "It didn't matter if they went with what I was wearing or even if they matched."

Kayla surreptitiously rubbed her knuckles over the

center of her chest. Jane had never mentioned that before, and she was sure that when she took over the little girl's care she'd likely done the barrette selection herself. "I wish I'd known," she said, touching the girl's hand. "I would have let you do the choosing, too."

Jane shook her head, her unfettered hair swirling around her shoulders. "It's all right. It wouldn't have been the same anyway."

No. And Kayla had never tried to mother them at the beginning. Aware that there wasn't a person who could step in and take on that role when they were still bewildered by their loss, she'd treated them more like an older sister would. Later, as time went on, she'd recognized her maternal feelings toward the kids, but had realized she couldn't expect them to ever feel toward her the reciprocal daughter-and-son sentiments.

"I really only remember her yellow sweatshirt," Lee suddenly said. "It was soft and the color of the sun, and I can picture her leaning over me at night to turn off the light and then tuck me in. Then I felt just as warm and happy as that sunny shirt."

Kayla froze. Oh. Oh, God. She knew that sweatshirt. Just as she knew the woman wearing it hadn't been Lee's mom. When she'd first started working for the family she'd worn her good-luck, high school sweatshirt over her T-shirt and jeans nearly every day. One of the school colors was egg yolk–yellow, and she remembered how much the little boy had loved it—even asked about it after she'd lost the thing during some park outing or another.

Meaning the memory Lee had of his mother was a memory of Kayla instead, which of course she could never say.

And she couldn't cry about it in front of him, either.

"Hair done?" she said, her voice tight but bright as she stood.

"I guess," Jane answered, moving back. "Though—"

"Though nothing. It's perfect." Kayla barely glanced at her reflection in the mirror. "I've got to get going so I'm ready for my evening out."

By breathing deeply, she made it to her room without emotion overcoming her. There, she sat on the edge of the bed, taking more steady breaths to keep herself from toppling onto the mattress and succumbing to sadness.

It hit her anyway, though, and it was then she remembered Mick's words she'd heard earlier that day.

We should be thinking about getting a new Kayla.

Now she thought she understood what he'd been getting at. He realized that she was too close to the kids. They weren't her children; she wasn't their mother, and forgetting that could end in heartache, especially for her.

The solution? As Mick had said, the family was going to need a new nanny. She would have to move on, to another family or another kind of situation. Soon.

Leaping to her feet, she decided to leave early for her dinner. She was still in her dress and boots from her lunch date so there was no need to change. It would be better to get out of the house ASAP and at least start pretending to have a good time. She grabbed her cell phone from the bedside table. It was in her hand as she rushed toward the front door. Mick was just stepping over its threshold.

"Dropped them off," he said, smiling at her. "On your way out to your birthday celebration?"

"Yeah." Her gaze shifted to her phone as it buzzed in her hand. An incoming text message. It only took a moment to read the short line.

To realize…

Mick put his hand on her arm. "Kayla? What's wrong?"

To her dismay, she burst into tears. Already in emotional overload thanks to Lee's memory of the sweatshirt and her awareness that she couldn't stay the family's nanny forever, the text message sent her straight over the edge.

Mick's grasp on her tightened. "Kayla?" he said again.

"There's not going to be a birthday celebration," she confessed. "I'm all dressed up with no place to go."

It was just like Mick had imagined a week before. A date scene. Small table covered in white cloth. Gleaming cutlery. A bottle of wine and two glasses.

Kayla's birthday dinner.

When she'd blurted out that she was all dressed up with no place to go, what other option had there been? Well, there'd been another option, that of him comforting Kayla in the now-childless house, and that had seemed like a terrible idea. Hell, terri*fying*.

So he'd handed her a handkerchief, quickly changed into slacks and a sports shirt, then hustled her out, driving them both to a spot where men took women who were dressed in pretty clothes and whose blond hair fell in a shining, touch-me waterfall. Sure, it was a date scene, but at least thirty inches of table-top separated them.

She was still just the nanny, he told himself.

Sad and in need of a friend, but just the nanny all the same.

He clinked the rim of his wineglass against hers as the waiter settled the bottle onto the table and then turned away. "What should we toast to?"

"Me not making such a fool of myself ever again."

Her waterworks had been brief, but their aftereffect had lasted long enough for him to get her to his car and to the restaurant with minimum protest. She sighed, obviously doubting the wisdom of it now. "I don't know why I let you take me here. I'm sorry, Mick."

"There's nothing to be sorry about." He sipped at the wine. "You comfort and care for my family every day. I don't mind offering a little of that back."

"You probably had plans for yourself tonight." The only evidence left of her emotional outbreak was the flush on her cheeks and clearly embarrassment had overcome her sadness.

"The only plan I had was kicking back in front of the TV. Fifteen minutes of that in a house without the kids and I would have been so bored I wouldn't know what to do with myself."

"Then maybe you would have popped up from the couch and done...I don't know. Something."

"Yeah, because I'm so impulsive like that."

She grimaced. "Funny, the kids and I were talking about impulsiveness today. I got to thinking about how less-than-spontaneous I am. Have you ever thought you could use a little recklessness in your life?"

"You, Miss Twentysomething, can be reckless," he said, pointing in her direction. "Me? Father of two? I'm better off being a stick in the mud."

Shaking her head, she smiled at him. The candlelight flickered, casting shadows under her cheekbones and bringing a sparkle to her big blue eyes. His gaze dropped to her mouth, her throat, and farther to her—no, that way lay danger. He forced himself to look back up.

"Mick…" she started.

"Mick…what?" He smiled too, now, pretending his attention hadn't wandered. "Mick, you're exactly right, you're one step away from the retirement home?"

"No." She laughed. "More like, Mick, you're an attractive, sexy guy who should—"

The waiter arrived with their meals and she stopped talking as he served their plates. Mick promised himself he would leave the rest of her sentence well enough alone. It seemed like a stupid idea to insist she finish her thought. *Mick, you're an attractive, sexy guy who should…*

Stop thinking sexy thoughts about the attractive nanny a mere thirty inches away.

The attractive, sexy nanny who would go home with him tonight to an empty house.

He tried drowning that small fact in a large swallow of wine. Then he applied himself to his food, letting silence fall between them until he could think of something besides dark rooms and satiny skin. *You're here for a reason,* he reminded himself. *Remember that friendly comfort you wanted to offer Kayla?*

"So what's going on?" he asked, putting that parental timbre into his voice he used when he was trying to shake down the kids for information on the source of a sibling squabble or what weekend homework was yet unfinished. "What upset you earlier? It was more than the canceled dinner."

She glanced up at him, then back to her food. "It's nothing."

"Kayla." He waited until she looked up again. "We're buddies, right? Let me help."

"Buddies." Her smile was rueful. "No. We're boss and employee."

"Not only that," he insisted. He didn't want to get more specific, he shouldn't get more specific, but he also couldn't let her get away without asking about those tears. "Face it. We're almost fam—"

"Don't say the word," she put in quickly. "Don't say family."

He raised an eyebrow. "Is this about yours and your birthday celebration that isn't?"

She sighed, then looked away, her fingers toying with the stem of her wineglass. "The truth is, I was supposed to be meeting an old friend. There was no birthday celebration planned with my parents and half siblings. They usually forget."

"About the date?"

"About me."

He attempted to keep up. "I'm aware your parents are divorced..."

"And when I was about Jane's age, each remarried and went on to have more children with their respective new spouse. I have seven half siblings. I'm the only one who is the product of my mother's and father's relationship."

"How does that explain forgetting your birthday?" He was a father. He had kids. How could you forget the date a child came into your life?

She shrugged. "Think about it. I'm the inconvenient one. The one that doesn't completely belong with either tribe."

Mick stared. "For God's sake, Kayla. That's not a reason to forget about you."

"It's no big deal. I understand it—I understood it

years ago. I remember when my dad was looking for a new job. It was right after I graduated from high school and he wanted to show me what a résumé looked like. The last line read, 'Married, with four children,' and there it was. He has four kids with his second wife. I wasn't one that counted."

Mick felt... Mick didn't want to feel. Maybe if he was just some guy, he could have adopted her casual attitude. But he was a father, and the idea of ever pretending, ignoring—what would you call it?—one of his children made his belly ache. And more...so much more, he hated the idea that Kayla had been hurt, no matter how she tried to dismiss it. Appetite gone, he pushed his plate away and saw that she'd already abandoned hers.

"Are you ready to head home, honey?" he asked, aware of the intimacy of the question and the tenderness in his voice, yet not regretting either.

"Yes," she said. "I'm ready."

His arm naturally went around her waist as they walked toward the exit once the bill was paid. In the foyer, he was surprised to find his friend and fellow firefighter Will Dailey. The other man stood beside his wife, obviously waiting to be led to a table. Mick's feet slowed as Will's gaze landed on the proprietary hand he had on the nanny.

Just the nanny, he reminded himself, letting his arm slide away.

Kayla knew Will and his wife, Emily. The station was another kind of family and she'd met those two at summer barbecues and at potluck dinners the station hosted for those working the holiday shifts. They exchanged a round of pleasantries, and Kayla expressed delight in the news that the other couple was expecting a baby. It was news to Mick, too. He clapped his buddy on the back and kissed Emily on the cheek.

It was Mick's wife, Ellen, who had wanted children early in their marriage. He hadn't objected, though honestly, he hadn't felt as compelled as his wife to start diapering so soon. Now, though, he couldn't imagine life without Jane and Lee. Not only because they were his remaining link to Ellen, but because… they were who they were. Because they made his life richer and brighter.

He grinned at Will. "You get to do Disneyland again," he said. "You don't know how much you've missed the magic of Mickey until you go back with your own little ones." That's what they did, he thought. Kids brought special magic into an adult's life.

A woman could do that, too, Mick realized, as he drove Kayla home. He breathed in her scent and the danger he'd felt at the beginning of the evening at the idea of being alone with her dissipated. It was pleasure he felt at her warm presence beside him. There was no denying the appreciation he had of her beauty, the loveliness he found in her silky hair, blue eyes, tender mouth.

The darkness closed around them, intimate and private, as they walked into the house. They came through the back door and into the kitchen, their feet pausing at that exact spot on the hardwood floor where he'd instructed her on how to kiss.

Her gaze turned up to his. A new tension rose, swirling as thick as the darkness and the unfamiliar quiet. He knew Kayla sensed it, too, because her voice turned breathless. "Well," she said, low and husky. "Well."

"Well," he whispered back, smiling a little. "Well."

Why had he been concerned about this closeness with her? he wondered. It seemed as unsurprising as it was easy now, a simple extension of all the ways they teamed together as a unit to keep their intertwined lives running smoothly. He almost laughed at himself at the thought, because did he really think it was so simple as breakfast, lunch, bed? But it *was* simple in that it didn't require anything but breathing

GET 2 BOOKS

THE WEDDING GIFT
SANDRA STEFFEN

L.A. CINDERELLA
AMANDA BERRY

We'd like to send you two *Silhouette Special Edition®* novels absolutely free.
Accepting them puts you under no obligation to purchase any more books.

HOW TO GET YOUR
2 FREE BOOKS AND 2 FREE GIFTS

1. Return the reply card today, and we'll send you two *Silhouette Special Edition* novels, absolutely free! We'll even pay the postage!

2. Accepting free books places you under no obligation to buy anything, ever. Whatever you decide, the free books and gifts are yours to keep, free!

3. We hope that after receiving your free books you'll want to remain a subscriber, but the choice is yours—to continue or cancel, any time at all!

EXTRA BONUS

You'll also get two free mystery gifts! (worth about $10)

FREE!

Return this card promptly to get
2 FREE BOOKS and 2 FREE GIFTS!

SPECIAL EDITION™

YES! Please send me 2 FREE *Silhouette Special Edition*® novels, and 2 free mystery gifts as well. I understand I am under no obligation to purchase anything, as explained on the back of this insert.

About how many NEW paperback fiction books have you purchased in the past 3 months?

❏ 0-2
E9S7

❏ 3-6
E9TK

❏ 7 or more
E9TV

235/335 SDL

FIRST NAME	LAST NAME

ADDRESS

APT.#	CITY

Visit us at:
www.ReaderService.com

STATE/PROV.	ZIP/POSTAL CODE

▼ DETACH AND MAIL CARD TODAY! ▼

(S-SE-10/10)

If offer card is missing, write to The Reader Service, P.O. Box 1867, Buffalo, NY 14240-1867, or visit www.ReaderService.com.

BUSINESS REPLY MAIL
FIRST-CLASS MAIL   PERMIT NO. 717   BUFFALO, NY

POSTAGE WILL BE PAID BY ADDRESSEE

THE READER SERVICE
PO BOX 1867
BUFFALO NY 14240-9952

NO POSTAGE
NECESSARY
IF MAILED
IN THE
UNITED STATES

for him to want her as he hadn't remembered wanting anyone before.

He'd been close to Kayla tonight, closer than he'd been to a woman in years and elevating that intimacy to another level seemed natural now, not problematic.

Maybe one day you wake up and look at someone you've known for a while and realize that the wow *is right there in the room with you both.*

Right now, something was in the room with them for sure. Desire. Need. Sex.

She was so damn irresistible, with her shiny blond hair, her sweet scent, her lovely eyes that he'd been staring into all night long. "God, Kayla."

"Mick…" Her gaze heated and he saw the same yearning on her face.

He cupped her head in his big hands. She made a sound low in her throat, and then there was no more thinking or considering or even second-guessing. Her mouth, so soft and luscious-looking, was impossible to turn away from. He found himself taking it, taking her into his arms, feeling her female shape against his body, tasting the warm, wet flavor of her mouth. God. God.

The quiet tightened around them. Their kiss deepened and she melted along his hard frame. The surrender of it galvanized him. Desire speared through him, a flame that burned and fired his need. His hands tightening on her, he backed her toward her room.

Her bed.

Once beside it, he had to be sure. "Kayla?"

"Yes," she said, answering his unspoken question. "I told you I need a little recklessness in my life."

Chapter Seven

A woman could want a warm body in her bed on her birthday, right? That it was technically the night before her birthday didn't matter. That it was technically Mick Hanson, not just some warm body, didn't matter, either.

Who was she kidding? That it was Mick Hanson only made it the best present ever.

She ignored any twinges of concern that this would change things forever between them. It didn't need to. And anyway, who could predict forever? Nothing was predictable except that at this moment she couldn't move away from Mick.

His mouth trailed across her cheek and down her

neck, inciting goose bumps and then chasing them with his tongue. Her pulse thrummed and her body shivered against his. "Cold?" he whispered.

She shook her head and ran her hands up his chest. His muscles, those hard muscles that she'd been watching for years as he walked half-naked up the stairway to his shower, hardened against her palm. She crowded closer, unable to help herself from pushing her belly against the stone strength of his sex. He groaned, his hips pushing back against hers. "Kayla, sweetheart. I want to take this slowly."

"No," she murmured, drawing his mouth back to hers. "Now. More." As sure that she couldn't predict forever, she also couldn't predict past the single instants ahead—the next kiss and then the next touch. If they lingered, she was afraid something would interrupt—conscience, kids, a call from the fire station.

The fragility of this moment, like a bath bubble floating in the air, only made her heart pump faster. Her mouth opened under his and her hands drew along the cotton of his shirt to his buttons. They clumsily unfastened them.

I ironed this shirt, she realized. She'd hung the pants he'd take off to take her. The thought made her fingers fumble. What was so familiar—his clothes, his body, his voice—would all take on a different kind of familiarity once they took this step.

The turn of her mind must have telegraphed to him. He lifted his head, his gaze trained on her face, his mouth curved in a half smile. With his thumb, he traced the wet surface of her bottom lip. "I want you," he said. "But only if—"

"I want you, too," she interrupted, determined again. She made a second awkward attack on his buttons.

He chuckled, a soft, sexy sound, then pushed her fingers away. "I'll do that."

"Okay." She reached for the zipper at the back of her dress.

His hand captured hers. "I'll do that, too."

In fact, he did it first. His mouth came back to the side of her neck as his fingers latched on to the tab of her zipper. The rasp of it sliding down sounded loud in the dark. Air touched her spine as the sides of her dress parted, and it felt like a succession of cool kisses. More of them tickled across her shoulders as Mick pushed the fabric over them and it dropped to the ground.

He shifted back to stare at her body.

Cool turned hot as she saw his gaze move over her white lacy bra and matching panties. With her high-heeled black boots, she supposed she didn't look much like a nanny at the moment. "Mick..." she whispered, shaking.

His callused palm cupped her cheek. "You're so beautiful," he said, then let that raspy skin move down her neck, across her throat and around to her fabric-covered breast. He rested his hand there a moment, and she felt her nipple tighten against the slight pressure as her heart pounded in insistence.

"Mick..." she said again, a longing note in her voice.

His fingers slid beneath her bra, the tips just brushing the aching center. She swayed toward him, anxious, needy, so ready for more. *"Mick."*

He took his touch away. She swallowed her moan because he reached around to unlatch her bra. It fell to the ground, the white startling against the shiny leather of her black boots. His gaze followed hers to the sight, then moved upward slowly, past her calves, her trembling knees, her thighs. His hand joined in, caressing her flank, then catching on the elastic edge at the top of her panties.

Just that, and melting heat flooded between her legs. She felt her flesh soften and swell. He stared at his long fingers as they toyed there, rubbing the lace, then sliding beneath to the tender skin covering her hipbone.

Kayla couldn't breathe. She couldn't think beyond *hurry. Hurry, hurry.*

But Mick was still in slow motion, and apparently mesmerized by his own hand or the feel of her flesh beneath it or both. Then he stepped close again. His cloth-covered chest brushed against her tightened nipples as he took her mouth in another possessive kiss. Both hands slid beneath her panties to grasp the globes of her bottom. She pressed herself against his erection, giving in to the kiss, giving everything she had to him.

Her panties skimmed down her thighs. At his urging, she found herself stepping out of them. Then he broke the kiss and moved away once more, and she realized she was naked—except for her knee-high black boots.

She wasn't the nanny anymore.

And she figured that's exactly what Mick wanted.

Even though she was as turned on as she'd been a moment before, she felt herself relax. Okay. Okay. From the avid look on his face, this wasn't something she had to rush through before the Cinderella spell was broken and they found themselves fully clothed and washing dishes or sweeping floors.

On a slow turn, she reached for the covers on the bed to draw them back. She could feel Mick's gaze on her backside, and she let herself picture what he did—her pale skin gleaming in the light filtering from the hall, her black boots with their darker, naughtier shine. The image paralyzed her for a moment, and then Mick was behind her, the crispness of his clothes brushing her shoulder blades and her bottom. His hand caressed her hip.

"I'll never look at boots the same way again," he said.

She titled her head to rest against his shoulder. He hadn't said he'd never look at her the same way again, but that wasn't the point. The point was, it was Kayla's birthday and he was her gift of the night.

His palms covered her breasts. With a gentle touch, he molded them, exploring their weight. When his thumbs brushed her nipples, she whimpered.

He kissed his way down her neck and his fingers plucked at those ruched tips, each little pinch tighter than the one before. She pushed back with her hips, loving the scrape of cloth against her, but wanting him naked even more. Her hands moved behind her and she yanked the tails of his shirt from his waistband.

"Get naked," she whispered, deciding a girl in black boots could give an order or two.

He laughed again, his breath warm against her throat. "If you get on the bed."

She did so, eagerly. He shed his shirt first. It fell on top of her discarded clothes and the mere symbolism of it goosed her with a little sexual thrill. His eyes narrowed at the shiver that ran through her. She thought his breathing moved in and out a little faster.

Then his hands shifted to the fastening of his pants. It took only a moment for him to shuck the rest of his clothing, and she was glad for it, because she couldn't find air in the time it took for him to get completely naked. Her heart shut down in anticipation. She'd seen him from the waist up. She'd seen him from the knees down. But now she had it all, including his long, muscled thighs and the matching erection already in its fully aroused state.

He set a condom on the bedside table—had it been in his wallet? His pocket?—then he crawled onto the bed, and her heartbeat restarted. Operating on instinct, she parted her thighs and he fastened his gaze on her slick center as he moved closer. "Kayla," he said, and two of his fingers reached out to skate over the swollen flesh. "You're so beautiful all over."

She was burning, that was sure. As he played with her drenched tissues, she sank deeper into the pillows. Her thighs opened wider, giving him more access. A finger slid inside and she gasped, her hips bowing. Mick glanced up. "I promise I won't hurt you. Just open up for me, baby."

He eased a second finger inside and the fit was tight. Deliciously tight. She writhed against them and then writhed some more as his thumb nudged the bud at the top of her sex. "Mick." Her head thrashed on the pillows and she reached out to palm his shoulder. "Please."

"Yes," he murmured. "I'll please you." And then he moved over her, taking a nipple in his mouth as his fingers continued to fondle her sex.

Her fists gripped the sheets. He plumped the other breast with his free hand and she went wild at the different caresses: the wet suction of his mouth, the tender touch on her breast, the insistent impalement of his thrusting hand and that arousing, knowing thumb.

When his mouth switched to her other nipple, when his fingers thrust and his thumb pressed one time, a second, she pushed into those maddening touches…and came.

Maybe he was maddened, too, because just as her quakes turned into shivers he slid his hand away and impaled her with something else instead. But he was going slow again, entering her in increments of inches, taking his time to fully seat himself. When he was inside her all the way, he groaned, and came down on her mouth in a hot kiss, his tongue thrusting.

She wrapped her legs around him, the leather of her boots sliding against his hips. It was another image she'd take with her forever and she held it in her mind as their bodies rocked into sweet, sweet oblivion.

When it was over, he rolled to the pillow beside her, and then rolled her against his side. She put her head on his shoulder and listened to the thudding beat of his heart. His hand made soothing passes along her upper arm as her gaze found the bedside clock. Midnight.

Happy birthday, she mouthed to herself. *Yes, indeed, you gave yourself quite the present.*

And she didn't regret a moment of it, even as things he'd said and promises she'd made to herself came back to her.

He'd said: *I'll please you.*

She'd thought: *Having sex wouldn't change things between them.*

He'd said: *I'll never hurt you.*

Ah, well. Of the three, she suspected only the first would stand the test of time.

In the morning, Kayla awoke to an empty bed and the sound of dishes clattering in the kitchen. Maybe it had been a dream, she thought for a moment, but then she spied her boots, left right where Mick had tossed them last night after they'd made love and before he'd pulled the covers around them.

Her skin heated at the memories and she wondered exactly how to handle this morning-after business. Without hiding, she decided, getting up and heading for the shower. She was twenty-seven and old enough, woman enough, not to slink around like she was ashamed or embarrassed. Checking herself in the mirror, she didn't blush at the fact that the pink shirt she wore with jeans was one button lower than usual, that she'd double-coated her mascara or that her mouth was still so red from his kisses that she didn't need lipstick.

Her head was high as she walked into the kitchen.

But her heart sank. Because there he was, like a hundred times before and yet it was like no other time before. His back was to her as he worked at the stove while wearing another pair of worn jeans and a ratty T-shirt that she should have consigned to the rag bag ages ago.

I could just rip it off him right now, she thought. Smooth over this morning-after business by smoothing her hands up the muscles of his back, only to smooth them down the front of his chest to the fastening of his pants.

Perhaps she made some sort of sound at that, because he glanced over his shoulder. Smiled.

"Sleepyhead." He said it fondly, as if she was Jane or Lee. "Happy birthday." Then he pushed a mug of hot coffee in her hand and pulled out a chair for her at the kitchen table.

Unsure what else to do, she sat, then couldn't help her own smile when he served her a breakfast plate: bacon, wheat toast, a pile of sunny scrambled eggs topped by a pink birthday candle.

Who wouldn't be in love with that? With him.

She was in love with Mick. She'd admitted that to herself over a week ago. Even though she didn't believe he reciprocated those feelings, that didn't mean they couldn't explore this new territory of their relationship, right? She'd gone into it as a one-night stand and she'd been afraid it would alter what they already had together...but was that such a bad thing? Couldn't they have an affair with the hope that it might lead to more?

She was old enough, woman enough, to express that plainly, right?

He was staring at her. "Well?"

Oh, God. Was she supposed to blurt it out right

now, right here, over scrambled eggs and strawberry jam? "Um...what?"

"Well, aren't you going to make a wish?"

"Oh." She relaxed against the back of the chair. "Sure." Closing her eyes, she tried formulating words that would express her greatest hope and her greatest fear.

Don't let what I say ruin anything.

The wish wasn't perfectly precise, but she blew out the birthday candle anyway.

Mick took the seat across from hers, and just as if it was any other day, he handed her the front section of the newspaper and picked up the sports page for himself. The only thing missing was the kids squabbling over who got the prize in the cereal box. Now it was her turn to stare. Did he really expect it to go like this?

After a moment, he glanced up. A wry smile flashed over his face. "Sorry. Am I doing it wrong? I'm not well-practiced in mornings-after."

"That makes both of us." She tried out her own little smile.

He folded up his section of newspaper. "Maybe we can muddle along together."

"We've managed to do that for the last six years, I guess." Surely they could muddle their way into an affair and then...

"Yeah." But his expression closed and he glanced away from her. "Kayla…"

Her belly hopped at the note of regret in his voice. She swallowed, though, determined to not let this chance pass by. "Let's be honest with each other, Mick."

"All right. I think that's a good idea."

"I know last night I said I wanted to be reckless, but it…" She was losing her nerve. "It didn't feel reckless with you."

He reached across the table for her hand. "I'll take that as a compliment. You mean a lot to me, Kayla."

It wasn't exactly a declaration on the scale of what she wanted to say to him, but still she steeled herself to put her heart on the line. "And Mick—"

"That's why I feel so guilty."

She stilled. "Guilty?"

"Guilty," he confirmed. "I've known something for more than a week, after a talk I had with Patty Bright. She, uh, told me something about you."

Heat washed up Kayla's throat. Patty Bright was a nice woman who had been close to Mick's wife. Had she detected Kayla's feelings for her friend's husband? It was one thing for her to tell him herself, but what if the two of them had been talking about the lovesick nanny? Maybe even laughing about the lovesick nanny.

Her stomach churned. "I don't know what she could know about me," she said. "We're only casual acquaintances."

Mick grimaced. "She knows you better than you might think."

So Patty had told Mick that Kayla had feelings for him and now he felt guilty because last night he'd come to her bed out of…what? Pity? At the thought, Kayla rocketed to her feet. "I think you've got the situation entirely wrong." To hell with honesty. And she didn't need to sit here and be humiliated. "I have to…get going. Do something. Visit my family."

He raised an eyebrow at the blatant lie. "What's got you running, honey?"

"I don't like Patty discussing me." Kayla's voice was as hot as her face.

"Only because she didn't want to poach without giving me a heads-up first."

"Huh?" Wait. "What?"

Mick sighed. "Sit down?"

Confused, she returned to her seat. "I don't understand what's going on."

"Because I've been holding back on you." He took a breath, blew it out. "Here goes. Patty wants you to go to work for her family."

That cleared up nothing. "I have a job. Here."

"But the Bright family has an opportunity to spend several months in Europe. They thought you might see it as an opportunity for yourself, as well."

Kayla blinked. Europe? With another family? Leave Mick and Jane and Lee?

We should be thinking about getting a new Kayla.

Now she thought she understood what he'd meant by that. And why he'd been floating the thought by the kids. If she went to work for the Brights, then the Hanson family would need her replacement.

But no one could replace Mick and the kids in *her* life!

"Is that what you want?" Even though her heart was going at a jackhammer pace, her voice sounded steady to her own ears. "For me to leave you?"

He closed his eyes for a moment, opened them. "What I want, Kayla, is…" His palm swiped across his face. "Look—"

"Honesty, remember?" Her heartbeat pounded so loud in her ears now she didn't know if she would hear his answer. "You promised to tell the truth."

He glanced away, then it was he who rose to his feet in an abrupt movement. "I want what I've always wanted. To raise happy and successful kids. Not to have that responsibility make me crack."

With jerky movements, he yanked open the dishwasher and loaded his plate and mug, then slammed the door shut. "Which means I want to keep all the damn balls I already have in the air."

He snatched the newspaper—unread, not that she planned on mentioning it—off the table and threw it into the recycle bin by the back door. "And not add yet another to the mess I'm already juggling." A drawer was shoved shut with the flat of his big hand. "I don't want to risk screwing everything up."

Then the frying pan landed with a clatter in the sink. "What I want, Kayla, is no more changes!" The faucet gushed on. "Is that so hellishly demanding of me?"

Kayla gasped. She'd never seen his temper flare like this before. Mick had a long fuse and he'd always managed to smother the spark before an explosion. But now he appeared a breath away from an authentic, man-size detonation.

With his back to her, he grasped the edges of the countertop. Those muscled shoulders she always so admired were tense beneath the thin cotton. "I'm sorry," he said after a moment. She heard him take in a long, audible breath, then blow it back out. "Really sorry. I don't know what's wrong with me."

She knew. Last night they'd upset the order. They'd

initiated an alteration that he didn't desire. Mick wanted a nanny, not a lover.

Meaning he definitely didn't want her in the same way that she wanted him—and he definitely didn't want to want her that way. There would be no affair with the possibility of something else altogether.

So she stood again. "I understand," she said. "I understand perfectly."

Mick spun around. "You can't. You don't. Because I don't even—" He broke off at the sound of the front door opening and children's footsteps clattering against the floorboards. Jane and Lee's father groaned. "Look—"

"I get the message," she told him, as the children's voices drew nearer. Whether he wanted her to leave his employment for Europe was unclear. But she knew perfectly well now that he didn't want their previous platonic relationship modified in the slightest way. "And I'm happy to reassure you. What's between you and me hasn't changed," she said. "And I'm quite okay with that."

It might not be honesty, but her birthday wish had come true—*Don't let what I say ruin anything*—if Mick's relieved expression told the truth that she hadn't.

Chapter Eight

Surely every parent had moments when they silently groaned at the untimely arrival of their beloved children. When assembling a tricycle, say, on Christmas Eve or when downing a spoonful of chocolate chip cookie dough straight from the tube. But this time Mick wasn't wielding a wrench or guiltily ingesting a concoction of uncooked eggs, flour and sugar. He was midway into discussing some serious subjects with the nanny.

With Kayla, whom he'd made love to the night before.

He glanced over at her as the kids came rushing into the kitchen and the closed expression on her face and her stiff posture told him everything he needed to know. He hadn't handled the morning-after thing well, not since he'd slid a breakfast plate under her pretty nose.

Damn him!

Last night had been... God, last night he'd been in bed with a naked woman wearing black leather boots! He hadn't even fantasized something so good since a million years ago before marriage and kids, and that it was Kayla's soft flesh and Kayla's sexy footwear only made it sweeter...and hotter.

The kids were chattering to them both about something and he pretended to listen as he cleaned up the pans. He'd fumbled presenting her the Europe opportunity, too. He could have mentioned it in a neutral manner, but the idea of her leaving them had singed the edges of his brain. So he'd ranted about change, stomped around like a two-year-old and generally made an ass of himself.

An ass she'd probably be happy to leave behind in the States when she went off to Europe with Poaching Patty and family.

Mick realized he was strangling a handful of cutlery, so he forced his fingers to relax and dropped them into the dishwasher. Okay, he had to calm down. He had to calm down and then talk to the nanny like a rational being and express to her that he was completely fine with her decision to leave them, if it came to that. And then he'd agree with her last statement to him. Sure, they'd been intimate last night, but that didn't mean anyone had to change their life over it.

He didn't *want* to change his life over it.

So he'd be sure the nanny understood that he understood that the joining of their bodies the night before hadn't created a snarl in their domestic lives that couldn't be loosened.

With that decision made, he interrupted Jane's blow-by-blow description of the movie she'd watched with her girlfriends the night before. "Kids, go up to your rooms and put your sleepover stuff away. Leave the sleeping bags beside the hall closet and I'll stow them on the shelf later."

"Daddy—"

"Now, Janie." He gave her the "or else" eye, which put a puzzled look on her face, mainly, he supposed, because he wasn't big on "or else" parenting. But she left the kitchen anyway, her little brother trailing behind her.

As soon as they were gone, he turned back to Kayla. "Listen…"

She was already on her way to her room. He leaped to catch her, managing to snag her arm. They both stilled. It was the first time he'd touched her since leaving her bed. At dawn, he'd come awake, and from the pillow beside hers, he'd stared at Kayla, taking in the tumbled hair, the mouth still swollen from his kisses, the feathery delicacy of her eyelashes. He'd looked at people sleeping before—had watched his kids' snoozing away a hundred times—but watching Kayla sleep had sent him straight into panic.

Because he'd wanted to wake her up and he'd wanted to watch over her sleep—in equal measure. He'd wanted her like a man wants a woman and wanted to protect her…like a man wants to protect a woman, too.

"Kayla." Looking down, he realized they were standing in that magic place again, the one that had been the site of their first kiss and then for their next one that had led them straight to her bed. "This spot has got to be like that phantom tollbooth or that oddly numbered railway platform."

She didn't laugh. The seriousness of her expression told him he'd really, *really* blown it before. But with her so close, he couldn't seem to think of the best way to make up for it. And then he realized she was trembling at his touch, and his chest started to ache again. "Kayla," he murmured, leaning down to kiss her.

"Dad!" At Lee's shout, Kayla jerked away from

him. Her arm slid through his grasp like water, leaving his hand open...and too empty.

"Dad." Lee's sneakers slid on the hardwood floor as he came to a stop. "Where's Goblin? We can't find her anywhere."

Mick stifled his sigh. "Are you calling for her? You know that sends her deeper into hiding." The perverse creature seemed to enjoy being elusive. "Remember, we have to trick her. If you go about your business, sure enough she'll show up."

"Why are girls like that?" Lee demanded.

Jane, stepping into the kitchen, scowled at her little brother. "Maybe because boys are so stupid. Always shouting and rough."

Mick winced, thinking of his clumsiness this morning. No wonder Kayla had tried to escape to her bedroom before he could clear things up with her. "Uh, let's not use the word *stupid,* okay, people?"

His daughter's face took on that teenish stubborn cast that made him dread the future. "But, Dad—"

"Jane, why don't you check the linen closet in your bathroom?" Kayla put in. "You know how Goblin loves to knock over the stacks of towels in there. Lee, you look under your bed."

The kids filed out of the room, distracted from an incipient argument. What would they do without Kayla? Mick wondered. Surely he'd need the nanny as teen hormones continued to rise. Only she could help him manage creatures he feared might start behaving like werewolves under a perpetual full moon.

But he wasn't supposed to be thinking of a future with Kayla in it, he reminded himself, as he heard the kids' footsteps on the stairs. He was supposed to be making it clear she'd was free of him and his family if that's the way she wanted it.

Turning to her, he started the discussion that had been interrupted before. "You need—"

She clutched his arm. "Mick," she whispered. "Did you bring in the cat last night?"

His eyes widened. Crap. *Crap.* Goblin had adopted them at approximately age one and she'd clearly been accustomed to being outdoors at least part of the day. They managed to get her in each night—though he didn't want to think about how often he'd had to wander around the yard to lure her from the darkness with a piece of cheese or salami. Yeah, she was a deli kind of cat. But last night...

"Last night I wasn't thinking of much besides..."

"I know." She bit her lip even as her grip tightened on his arm. "We should have remembered, though. Think of all those gruesome coyote stories we've heard."

He saw her shudder. "It's going to be okay. We'll fan out, find her safe and sound somewhere."

Although she nodded, her face looked miserable. The ache in his chest sharpened. "Honey," he said, tucking her hair behind her ear. The strand was silky and her skin so soft beneath his fingertips. It was bad of him, he knew it, but he bent and left a swift, hard kiss on her mouth. "We'll handle it."

"Okay." She nodded again. "Okay. We always handle what comes, don't we?"

"Yeah, but—" Then the kids were there again.

"No Goblin," they said together, both small faces worried.

Mick slapped his hands together. "Let's go track her down, then. Backyard, front yard. After that, we'll hit the sidewalk if she hasn't shown up."

She didn't show up.

Thirty minutes passed and they had to conclude that the cat either wasn't nearby or she wasn't coming out of hiding even for turkey bologna or a slice of Monterey Jack. "Damn it," he murmured to Kayla. "Really, does she have to be this difficult?"

"Are you talking about me, Daddy?" Jane demanded, popping up at his elbow.

He was not going to survive to see her at seventeen, he thought, pressing his fingers to his throbbing temple. And then Lee was tugging on the hem of his shirt. "Promise me, Dad," his son said, with tears in his eyes. "Promise me we'll get Goblin back."

A hammer went to work on Mick's other temple. It was a parent's nightmare, being asked to make promises he knew he couldn't guarantee. "Sure, son," he said, pulling the little kid close. And then Jane did one of her child-teen turnarounds and threw herself against him, too.

Kayla stood nearby, looking just as glum as the kids. Without a second thought, he scooped her into the family embrace. He didn't feel guilty about it, not for a second, even though he realized a group hug wasn't the best way to untangle the new knot of intimacy they'd recklessly created the night before.

After the upheaval of the past week—the unsatisfactory aftermath of the night with Mick, the unsettling news of the European nanny job, the continued and upsetting absence of Goblin the cat—it became clear to Kayla that she needed to find ways to loosen her ties to the Hanson family. When Joe Tully, her recent blind date, had called yet again, she'd stopped making excuses and agreed to go out with him again.

Maybe she'd been wrong about her feelings for Mick.

And maybe *wow* could arrive on the second date.

She drove to the restaurant under her own steam, unwilling to introduce Joe to the Hanson family. Tonight was supposed to be about distancing herself from them, and she tried envisioning each block was a mile as she drove to a local seafood-and-steak place that she'd suggested. As she walked inside, she smoothed her soft, printed skirt and checked that the thin cardigan she wore with it was buttoned securely to the throat.

Her date stood up and kissed her cheek when she found him in the bar. Joe was not yet thirty and he wore a pair of flat-front khaki pants and a knit shirt that displayed an impressive breadth of shoulder and well-developed biceps. His medium brown hair was clipped short, he had friendly green eyes, and he smelled like an insert in a men's magazine.

"I'm glad we could finally get together again," he said, as they took their seats and the waitress settled them with drinks on small square napkins. "I thought we might not have a chance before I had to go out of town again."

"My calendar has its own limitations," she said. "I work around a firefighter's schedule, meaning there are stretches when I'm responsible for the kids twenty-four hours a day."

"But you said it was a good position for you while

you were going to college. Now that you have your degree are you going to use it?"

She'd thought she might. Teaching or counseling at the elementary level held a definite appeal, although each would require more schooling. "I haven't been considering much beyond my next homework assignment and the family's next load of laundry for so many years that it's hard to wrap my mind around the future."

"You could do anything," Joe said. "Think about it, you're young, healthy, single. Though I sometimes complain about all the travel I do for my job, most of the time I really enjoy it. Highly recommend seeing as much as you can of wherever you can afford to go."

Like Europe. At twenty, she'd taken off for the summer and bummed around several western European countries. Everyone she'd told about it before or since assumed it was the adventure of a lifetime—and she had taken pleasure in seeing sights that she'd only read about before. But she'd also experienced a heavy sense of loneliness as she wandered down the streets of London and the lanes of Provence. Adventures—at least for her, she realized—needed a partner and she hadn't been able to shake the notion that if she'd disappeared in the middle of Covent Garden that no one would have noticed...or cared.

Upon coming home, she'd almost immediately made herself indispensable to the Hansons. But sometimes she wondered who needed whom the most.

This night was supposed to take her away from them and those kinds of thoughts. So she pasted on a friendly smile and encouraged Joe to tell her his favorite travel destinations. He was waxing on about a trip to the Florida Keys when her chair was bumped by someone heading for a bar stool. "I'm sorry," the woman automatically said, but then she paused. "Kayla! Hey, good to see you."

Marcia Wells was a young mother she knew from Jane and Lee's elementary school and whose dimples dug deep when she smiled. Usually she was dressed in bright workout gear, but now she had on dark jeans and a pretty blouse with silk ruffles around the plunging neckline.

"You and Wayne are out on the town tonight?" Kayla guessed.

The other woman wiggled in a little jig, her high heels tapping on the floor. "Date night with my hubby. Moms like us don't get many of those—" She broke off, obviously realizing a moment late that Kayla wasn't anyone's mother. Her gaze jumped across the table to handsome Joe. "Um, it looks like you're having a good time, too."

Kayla made the obligatory introductions. "Marcia

and I served on the Faculty Follies PTA committee," she explained to Joe.

"We were in charge of the refreshments last year. This girl and I make a mean fruit punch," Marcia boasted, her dimples flickering again. Then her gaze caught on a figure entering the bar. "Here's Wayne now. You two have a good time!"

"Likewise," Kayla murmured to the woman's retreating back. Then she glanced at Joe, who was studying her with a new intensity, his green eyes narrowed. "Um? Do I have margarita salt on my nose?"

He shook his head. "Nah. I'm just catching on to what you do, is all. You're not just the nanny. You don't just babysit those kids."

She shrugged, for some reason embarrassed. "So I serve on a PTA committee or two."

"I don't even know what PTA stands for."

"You'll find out someday, I'm sure," she said.

Now it was his turn to shrug. "I'm in no hurry, believe me. My brother has kids and all he does is tell me about how much they cost and how they can't even walk down the street by themselves. He's trying to channel our dad who laid down the law and woe to he who broke a single one."

Kayla tried not to frown, but Joe's brother sounded, frankly, like a jerk. Mick had never complained about the expense of raising Jane and Lee. He was a protective father, that was true, but he gave them opportunities to walk down the street and venture on other independent experiences without heavy-handed supervision. And while her own father had been good with laying down the law those weekends she'd spent with him as a child, through them she'd come to realize there was more to being a parent than rule-making. He'd been absolutely clueless about her emotional landscape.

Mick got his kids, even though he was wary of what lay ahead as Jane and Lee approached their teen years. She was convinced he'd do a good job navigating troubled waters, with or without her.

Without her. Remember? Tonight was supposed to be about their life without her—or more correctly—her life without them. So she spread another smile across her face and asked Joe about his car.

He liked to talk about his car.

The meal was delicious, though she kept sneaking glances at her watch. *Was this any way to look for* wow? she admonished herself, even as she peeked at it again. But the whole evening felt more like *whatever,* she realized, as she ordered coffee to keep him company as he ate dessert.

It was not that there was anything wrong with Joe. Enjoying travel and a single's lifestyle or expressing an uncertainty about wanting children wasn't egregious. She knew all this. It was unreasonable of her to think a man unwilling to commit to a kid didn't make good date material. But…

You get to do Disneyland all over again.

She remembered Mick saying that to his friends Will and Emily when they'd shared the news they were pregnant. Kayla understood the sentiment. Through the kids she enjoyed…well, to be honest, maybe she enjoyed the childhood she hadn't experienced.

Joe wasn't obligated to feel or appreciate the same, but at twenty-seven, should she spend her free hours with someone who didn't share her interests or focus?

Her watch didn't have the answer, but she took another glance at it anyway, frowning to see how slowly the minutes ticked by. Maybe something was wrong with it. With a vague feeling of unease tickling the nape of her neck, she excused herself.

On the way to the ladies' room, she dug into her purse for her cell phone and powered it on. Four missed calls from Mick. Her breath hitched, then she thumbed the dial button.

He picked up. "Having fun?" The light question sounded forced.

Her breath hitched again. "What's wrong?"

"Nothing. I...um, had a little moment earlier, but it's all under control now."

"'A' little moment? You called four times within ten minutes, Mick."

"Yeah, well. About that. Three of those were Lee using my phone before I stopped him. The last one was me."

"What's wrong?" she asked, repeating herself.

"Nothing. Nothing that should interrupt your evening with...uh, Jonah? Jasper?"

"Joe."

"Well, nothing should interrupt your evening with Joe. So go back to—"

"He drives a sports utility hybrid," she said quickly.

Mick was silent a moment. "Ah."

"It gets fifty miles to the gallon and has headlamp washers."

"Um," Mick said. "Green and clean."

"He doesn't think he ever wants children."

"That's not a crime."

"I keep telling myself the same." Then she hesitated. "For dessert, he ordered apple pie with whipped cream, not ice cream."

Another silence came over the line. "Well, that *is* a felony in my book."

"Mine, too," she admitted. Her hand tightened on the phone. "Why'd you call, Mick?"

She could practically hear the gears in his head turning. It took a few moments, then he finally spoke. "Could you come home, Kayla? We have a little emotional emergency on our hands."

Joe accepted her sudden defection with good grace, though she hardly took the time to assess his reaction. While she was glad Mick made clear that no one's physical health was at stake, the words "emotional emergency" had her heart pumping double time anyway.

He was waiting for her on the front porch, his hands stuffed in the pockets of his scarred leather bomber jacket. The jeans he wore had a paint stain on the knee from the time he'd helped her refurbish an old bookcase she'd found for her room. His chin was stubbled with whiskers he hadn't bothered to shave on his day off.

She ran up the walkway, desperate to cross the distance. "What's going on?" she demanded.

They stood beneath the porch light. Six months ago, she recalled, he'd found her in this exact position with that other fix-up date Betsy had talked her into. Instead of retreating to the house, he'd stood sentry, waiting for her to say goodbye and go inside. She'd felt...something vibrating off him then. Awareness? Maybe a little jealousy?

There was a mix of both in his gaze now. "Kayla. I shouldn't have—"

"Mick." She took two handfuls of leather and gave his jacket a little shake. "I'm here now."

"Yeah, but I shouldn't have imposed. I realized that the second after I hung up. You didn't answer when I called back."

"Because you couldn't have kept me away." So much for distance.

One hand emerged from his pocket and he brushed his thumb against her bottom lip. She shivered, and only barely stopped herself from tasting him with her tongue. "I'm having that same problem myself," he murmured.

Then his hand dropped as he sighed. "Are you prepared for a memorial service, honey?"

Chapter Nine

Mick had a secret. As a firefighter he'd walked into many gruesome, tragic scenes. He'd seen people's worlds shattered due to loss of property or loss of limb or life. He remained stoic and focused when on the job. It was only afterward that he'd have nightmares. For a few weeks following a particularly disturbing situation he'd endlessly dream of singed teddy bears or small, single sneakers in the middle of a highway.

He suspected many of his colleagues suffered similar symptoms and didn't talk about them—but the nightmares weren't his secret.

What Mick never let anyone know was how one

of those terrible events could make him around his kids. Watching them suffer an emotional blow while he was still undergoing the aftereffects of a stressful shift at work could bring him to his knees. He figured he'd be father toast if they ever figured it out. Dad having a bad day? Put on a sad face and he'd promise you the world to make it all better.

Two nights before they'd responded to a motor vehicle collision. A family in a compact, a guy in a construction rig. Two kids had been hurt, their mother killed. Mick didn't think he'd be sleeping well for the next month.

So when he'd caught a tear-stained Lee calling Kayla while she was on her date, Mick had found himself pretty desperate for another adult. Someone who would help him deal with what his kids had been planning since dinner. But now, faced with Kayla's concerned expression and taking in her date wear of skirt and sweater, he just felt guilty.

"You should go back to him," he said. "Finish your evening."

She crossed her arms over her chest. "Certainly not. What is this about a memorial service?"

Images flashed through his mind. The mangled car of two nights ago morphed into the car that Ellen had been driving the night she died. He remembered the bewildered expressions on his children's faces during their mother's funeral and then Lee's heartfelt distress tonight when Goblin was again a no-show for dinner.

"They want to hold a service for the cat," he explained. "A goodbye to Goblin."

"Oh, Mick."

"Yeah." He sighed. "Lee said he couldn't sleep without doing something. It was all Jane's idea." And Papa the Pamperer couldn't deny them a thing when he was under the influence of those black, sleepless nights. "You don't need to be invol—"

She was already walking through the front door. "Lee?"

The little boy rushed from the kitchen and into her arms. "La-La," he said, burying his face against her. "She didn't come home for dinner again. We don't think Goblin is *ever* coming home."

Mick felt his chest tighten. He thought his son was right and it was killing him. Kayla ran her hand over Lee's hair and looked over to meet Mick's gaze. The tears in her eyes only made him feel more like a louse. "I'm sorry," he mouthed. She deserved her evening out and he'd drawn her back to this.

"What do you and Jane have planned?" she asked Lee, her voice soft, her hand gentle on his head.

The boy's arms tightened on the nanny's middle. "We'll go outside with candles and stuff and talk about what a good cat she was. About how much we loved her."

Jane emerged from the kitchen. "Daddy, can you turn the speakers on outside so we can play Goblin's favorite song?"

"Sure." He would sing it himself—and he couldn't carry a tune in a paper bag—if he had to. "Uh, what *is* her favorite song?"

"That old one from the Christmas CD. 'Baby It's Cold Outside.'"

Dean Martin. And Deano's voice had Mick almost crying as they trooped into the chilly winter air, all of them bundled in coats. Kayla had helped Jane with the final preparations. On the round patio table sat a fat pillar candle. Its flicker added to the soft lighting from the landscape fixtures. The burly oak in the backyard stretched over them, its leafless eeriness adding to the somber mood.

"So how do we proceed, Jane?" Kayla asked, her voice hushed.

His daughter, who'd been businesslike during the organization of the ceremony, now hesitated. She shoved her hands in the pockets of her faux-fur-edged jacket. Then she looked over at Mick. "Daddy?"

Oh, God. He remembered the first night she'd sneaked into his room after Ellen was gone. He'd been trying to read in bed, when he'd really just been staring at the black squiggles on the white page. Looking up, he'd spotted a tiny, white-gowned ghost in the doorway. His heart had jolted, then his daughter's voice had called his name, breaking in just the way that it did now.

"Daddy, I miss her."

Then, like now, he opened his arms for his daughter. "Come here, baby."

She burrowed against him and Mick closed his eyes for a moment, wishing, as he had then, too, that he could absorb all her pain. Across the table, Kayla took Lee's hand in hers. "Shall we start?" she asked the boy, as Dean warbled about going away.

Mick's son nodded. "Goblin had beautiful yellow eyes and the fluffiest black fur."

"Remember when she first showed up?" Kayla prompted.

"She was thin and didn't have a lot of hair."

"That's right. And we went around and asked all the neighbors if she belonged to them and one called her, 'That ugly little thing.'"

"Her fur grew and turned shiny once we started feeding her," Jane put in.

"Maybe we fed her a little too much," Mick added. "But she'd yowl once her bowl of dry food was down by half. When we'd gone through that first bag of crunchy stuff the vet said we'd better put her on the low-calorie version."

"Probably because she was still supplementing with lizards," Kayla groused.

That surprised a laugh out of Lee. "La-La, you're such a big chicken. You sent me into the pantry with a broom to chase out the last one she trapped in there."

Kayla sniffed. "Because I was dealing with the twitching tail the reptile dropped to get away from her."

"You called Dad at work," Jane said, pointing at the nanny. "And said there was nothing in the nanny rule book about handling scaly stumps. You put a box over it and he had to throw it away once he got home after his shift was over."

"I was only making your father feel useful," Kayla said, straightfaced. "And Goblin enjoyed playing watch-cat on the box all afternoon."

There was a long moment of silence. "Goblin watch-catted me at night," Lee said. "I'd wake up and not feel scared or alone because she'd be on the pillow next to mine."

How often did his son need company in the dark? Mick wondered, regret swamping over him again. With his job, he wasn't always there to reassure his little boy.

Kayla gathered him close. "Yes, but you know you only have to call out and your dad will come, or if he's not home, you know I am. You're always safe, Lee."

"I know."

The grip on Mick's heart eased a little. "Always safe, buddy."

His son looked to his sister. "Now, Jane?"

She nodded. "Okay."

The boy detached himself from the nanny and headed to the house. He was back in a moment, balancing a paper plate in his hand. His movements solemn, he set it on the patio table. "Goblin's favorite treats," he said.

Mick's eyebrows rose. The cheese and salami were no surprise. But there was also a pile of taco-flavored corn chips, a tablespoon of ice cream and three pitless black olives.

The cat must have spent its days at the Hanson house suffering from serious indigestion.

"Thank you for your time with us," Lee said, looking into the darkness and taking Kayla's hand. "You were a nice cat."

"A pretty cat." Jane took her brother's hand and then Mick's.

"Who started scraggly," he added.

The candlelight flickered over Kayla's face. "But

who turned out to be as beautiful on the outside as she was on the inside."

Mick reached for her hand to complete the circle. It felt so small and fragile in his hold, hardly bigger than Jane's. That's how this moment felt to him, he thought—fragile, small, but important in a way he couldn't explain. Because their connection to the nanny felt so temporary now?

Jane sighed. "She needed a family."

"She needed us," Lee corrected.

"She did," Kayla agreed softly, her fingers tightening on Mick's.

He was going to lose it, he thought. He was going to lose it in front of his kids and all because it was hitting him from a thousand different directions that everything he held so dear was so transitory. The cat left their lives, the kids became independent, the nanny moved on to somewhere else.

Someone else.

He closed his eyes.

"What's the matter, Daddy?" Jane said.

"Moment of silence," he quickly put in. "Let's all close our eyes for a moment of silence."

He counted off the seconds in his head, giving himself a full sixty in which to get a grip. At forty-five, his daughter shrieked. He started, then stared.

Goblin. The damn cat was on the tabletop, lapping delicately at the melting ice cream.

Everyone else came alive, too. While they petted the missing feline, she continued eating, unperturbed. Then Jane hugged Kayla. Lee hugged him. Mick was left looking at the nanny.

And as if it was the most natural thing in the world, they went into each other's arms. "I'm glad you were here," he said, against her soft, fragrant hair. "I thought this was going to be a disaster."

"As usual," she murmured, "we muddled through."

"And found our way to triumph," he finished.

How much better, he realized, each of those could be with this woman in his arms.

The night of Goblin's reappearance strengthened the bonds between everyone in the Hanson household, Kayla thought, as she dusted the living room furniture early one morning before the kids left for school and before Mick returned home from his twenty-four-hour shift at the fire station. Jane and Lee were doting on the cat; Kayla and Mick were smiling at each other again. Not in the old way— there was still that simmering sexual tension beneath the surface—but she thought they were both more accustomed to the feeling now. Neither had broached the subject about what they should do about it. She figured they both accepted it wasn't going to up and evaporate.

For her part, when Joe Tully had called again, she'd made it clear there wouldn't be another date. However, she had agreed to a lunch with the Bright parents after finally speaking to Patty about the nanny position. While she'd been polite but also up-front about not being seriously interested in the offer, they'd insisted on taking her out for a meal to discuss it. She'd decided not to mention it to Mick, who hadn't brought up the idea of her leaving the family since her birthday.

Hope was blossoming again that she'd have everything she'd ever wanted. Even though she felt Mick struggling to keep his distance, that magnetlike tension between them made her believe he couldn't hold out for long.

Against her hip, her cell phone vibrated, and she dug it out of her jeans pocket. She glanced at the screen. The man himself.

"Good morning," she said.

"It's morning anyway," he answered, his voice weary. "Everything okay there?"

"Yeah." Was he aware that he always called home at the end of a particularly grueling shift? "Tough one for you?"

"Hearing your voice helps. Talk to me so I stay awake on the drive home. Do you need anything at the grocery store? I can stop on the way."

"We've got what we need, but thanks for asking. Well, unless you can find in one of the aisles the spelling worksheet Lee thinks he left in his desk at school yesterday."

"The one I suppose is due today but he's yet to finish."

"You're so smart," Kayla said, laughing. She ran the dust cloth over the surface of an end table.

"My son, on the other hand…"

"Has already figured out a work-around. He'll beg Ms. Witt to let him stay in at recess to finish up and he's counting on his charm and good looks to win her over."

Now it was Mick's turn to laugh. "Uh-oh. Should I claim he gets that confidence from dear old dad or not? Fact is, it sounds like you had a hand in that suggestion, La-La."

It was a childish nickname, *Lee's* nickname for her, but when Mick used it now, his low voice rasping in her ear, warmth flooded Kayla. Since she'd started the job, they'd talked on the phone often, but these days the calls held a new intimacy. If he'd been in the room he would see the flush on her face and perhaps sense the other physical effects he had on her. Even miles away with only his voice touching her, she felt her skin ripple with sensitivity and her nipples tighten.

"Cat got your tongue?" he murmured.

The warmth turned to heat and she shivered. The tongue in question was stuck to the roof of her mouth. "Mick…" she managed to get out.

"You said my name just like that the night in your bed," he said, his voice even raspier now. "When you begged me to take you over."

Oh. Her body softened for him and between her thighs a pulse started to throb. "Bad man," she protested.

"After a night like tonight, that's what I ache for, honey. To be your bad man."

"No fair," she whispered. "You're in a car by yourself, while I'm here at home—"

"Just steps away from that bed where we were naked together. Don't believe I haven't been thinking of it. I remember the exact scent of the skin along your collarbone. I know the taste of the slope of your breast. I can close my eyes and feel the way your body clasped my fingers when I slid them inside you."

"Don't close your eyes now," she said, her laugh shaky as hot waves of desire crashed over her. "I don't want you getting in an accident."

"Me neither. I want to be all in one piece once the

kids get off to school this morning and we're home alone together."

Lust nearly swamped her this time. "Mick," she groaned. Had the dam between them finally broken? He'd been so careful about keeping his distance and now he seemed ready for that closeness she needed.

"I don't know about you," he said, "But I can't deny myself any longer. I want to be in your arms again if you'll have me."

Giddy with pleasure, she reached out blindly, hoping to clutch the mantel to steady her now-shaky knees. Her fingers brushed one of the photos propped there and it fell, hitting the brick hearth with a loud crash. Kayla gasped, then stared down at the broken glass and mangled frame in dismay.

"What happened?" Mick asked, his voice sharp. "Are you all right?"

"I...I knocked over a photograph. It broke."

She could hear the relief in his voice. "That's okay, then. No harm done."

Kayla shook her head back and forth, her stomach queasy. "It's the picture of Ellen that was sitting on the mantel, Mick. I'm so sorry. I'm so very, very sorry."

He was quiet a moment. "Honey..."

"I would never do anything intentionally to...to...

damage it. Honest, Mick. I know you love her. I know how much you must miss her every single day."

He was silent again. "Kayla—"

"I can't believe I was so careless as to break it. The frame's probably irreparable and the glass is just slivers, but the photograph itself is fine." She knew she was babbling but she couldn't seem to stop. "I'll take it to the framer's and I'm sure they can take care of it in no time. No time at all…" Embarrassed, she forced herself to wind down.

"I'm sorry," she finally said again.

"Me, too," Mick said. "You realize you're over-reacting."

"No! Yes. Well…" She blew out a breath of air. "I feel really bad."

"Likewise." Mick blew out a matching audible breath. "I should have talked to you about Ellen before."

"She was your wife. You love her and you always will. I get all that." Kayla went to the utility closet to grab the hand broom and dustpan.

"I don't think you do, honey, and that's my fault."

Tucking the phone between her ear and shoulder, she cleaned up the mess and then carefully laid the photo on the coffee table. "You're not to blame for anything, Mick."

"Listen. This...thing between us has nothing to do with Ellen. She's been gone a very long time and maybe if I hadn't had the kids...but I did, thank God, and because of them I managed to drag myself through the dark times and into brighter days. The days are very bright now, Kayla."

She sank to the couch, her gaze on Ellen's smiling face. "That's good to hear, Mick."

"So you're probably wondering why I..." He released another breath. "It's not grief or fear of loss keeping me from another woman...from you. From your bed."

Her hands twined in her lap. "So what is it? After that night you didn't seem ready to, uh, repeat the event. Until this morning. Until now."

"Oh," he groaned. "If you only knew how ready I've been to repeat the event. Again and again and again. A guy can only hold off for so long."

"Then why..."

"Baby, I don't want to hurt you." She heard the worry in his voice. "And I don't know if I think..."

"You're thinking too hard, then," she said, concerned that he was ready to renege. Mick was slipping into protector mode and she didn't want him to be her hero, but her lover.

What came after that? Was there a future for them? She wanted that, but unless he allowed himself to get close to her again they both wouldn't know if it could really work. "You let me worry about myself. I've been on my own for a long time and I'm pretty good at it."

"Kayla—"

"The nights have been lonely for me, too, Mick. Come home. Come home and let's be company for each other."

"Oh, baby." There was a new lightness to his voice. "You're sure?"

"So sure, Mick. So sure."

He clicked off, saying he needed all his concentration now and she put her phone back in her pocket, her smile as wide as piano keys. Yes! Then she hopped up, wondering if she had time to do a once-over in her room and bathroom before he arrived and the kids left for school. Her gaze caught on the photo and she paused.

Thank you, Ellen, for sharing them with me. I won't let any of them down.

Especially when it was so close, she thought, to the four of them merging into something new and stronger than before. "I'm loving them for you," she whispered.

Footsteps on the staircase had her turning around. Her mouth gaped. Jane wore a micro-mini skirt in black. The hot-pink tights beneath it were the only thing keeping her from indecent exposure. But the top she wore with it—vaguely corset style that laced up the middle—looked like something worn by a desperate woman on a street corner.

The black of the ugly platform shoes on her feet was matched by the liner that ringed her eyes. Blue eyeshadow and hot-pink sticky lip gloss completed the ensemble.

"Is this a, uh, costume?" Kayla asked, vaguely gesturing at the girl's clothes.

"No." Jane didn't do an eye roll, but it seemed like a close thing. "I borrowed some things from Maribeth."

"Ah." Maribeth had been shaving her legs since fourth grade and wearing makeup since fifth. Mick and Kayla had agreed that sleepovers at Maribeth's weren't a good idea for Jane, although they'd welcomed the other girl to their house more than once. Her bag was always packed with celebrity magazines and lots of hair products.

When Jane reached the bottom of the stairs, Kayla saw that she was wearing every bracelet she owned on her right wrist. On her left she'd twisted a white bandana printed with tiny black hearts.

"Cute scarf," she said, nodding at it. She decided the multi-bracelets look wasn't a problem either, not in the grand scheme of things. "But you're going to have to wear a different top—how about that white long-sleeved T-shirt of yours—and Jane, you know you can't wear makeup to school."

The girl stiffened, her expression shocked. "What?"

Kayla wondered if she'd really expected to get away with breaking the house rules. Recalling the angst of preteenhood, she softened her voice. "Janie—"

"Jane."

"Jane. You know that I can't let you wear makeup."

"All the girls are wearing it today." The girl's voice was hostile. "We made a pact."

"I'm sorry, but—"

"You're not sorry! You're just being mean."

Kayla gazed on her young charge, remembering that just last night they were snuggled on the couch talking to each other in the funny voice they consigned to Goblin.

Humans, you are beneath me.

You are so lucky I decided to stay and rule your world.

The one with a queen complex right now was Jane. "Sweetheart—"

"I'm not listening to you." The girl brushed past.

Kayla grabbed for her arm. "Jane, you must go

upstairs and change your shirt and clean off that makeup."

At her touch, Jane yanked away. "I won't. I won't ever listen to you!"

"Come on—"

"You can't tell me what to do!" the girl shouted. "You're not my mother!"

The words pierced Kayla's chest. "Jane—"

"You'll never be my mother!"

"Jane."

"Go away," the girl said, bursting into tears. "Go away and stay there!" Then she stomped past Kayla and ran back up the stairs.

She stared after the preteen, until a new noise caught her attention. Before she turned she knew who stood there, she knew who'd witnessed the entire ugly debacle.

You're not my mother. You'll never be my mother! Jane had said. *Go away and stay there!*

And the girl's father, the head of the three-person unit that she longed to make into a foursome, the man she wanted to be beside forever, hadn't said a word.

Chapter Ten

Mick acknowledged he'd screwed up big-time as he returned home after driving the kids to school. When he'd walked in on his daughter's mini explosion, he'd not taken charge as he should have. Fatigue from the previous night, surprise at her astonishing outfit and a certain fuzziness brought on by a recent phone call that had fogged his windows were the culprits, he decided.

And now that blame for his inaction had been assigned, a solution must be identified.

He must contrive some way to make it up to the nanny.

The house was quiet when he let himself back

inside. Not one noise gave away where he'd find Kayla. Stymied, Mick stood in the living room, and his gaze caught on the photo of his wife on the coffee table.

He moved closer to it, staring into her dark eyes. He saw Lee in the shape of her face and Jane in the deep bow of her upper lip. *I'm putting them first,* he assured Ellen. *And I won't let the teen years get the best of me.*

The mistake he'd made this morning was in being unprepared for the outburst. It felt like another load of bricks on his shoulders, but he realized he'd have to be prepared to handle Jane's growing pains on a moment's notice if he was going to keep the rest of the household happy at the same time. He couldn't let his daughter hurt Kayla's feelings again.

He was pretty sure *he'd* hurt Kayla's feelings. There had to be a way to handle that, too.

Without caffeine, though, his brain started to spin. So he made his way to the kitchen, where he found the nanny sitting at the kitchen table, studying the newspaper. In her usual jeans and blouse, Kayla appeared relaxed. Yet her mood was impossible to gauge as she looked up. "No mishaps on the drop-off?" she asked.

"None." He beelined for the coffeemaker and the

empty mug sitting there. "Let me apologize for my daughter."

Her mouth twisted. "You don't need to do that."

"I do. She's my responsibility and she was way out of line this morning."

"She washed off the makeup."

"Yeah." He sighed. And she'd changed her clothes. The only thing of Maribeth's she'd kept on was the clunky-heeled shoes. All the jewelry had stayed as well, but bracelets were no big deal in his book.

The coffee went down hot and strong. He felt marginally better as the caffeine hit the bottom of his belly. "I think she's channeling Goblin."

Kayla, to his surprise, burst out laughing. "I had the same thought."

His mood easing, he pulled out the chair beside hers. "I'm thinking all those princess flicks we took her to as a little kid were not a good idea."

"I'm not sure a moratorium on movies would stop the inevitable, Mick."

"Change," he muttered under his breath. "Yeah, I get that. And I get that I have to deal with it. I'll go completely gray by forty, but I'll manage."

Kayla's hand covered his on the table. "You don't have to do it alone, Mick."

He looked over at her. "It's my job."

"Mine, too," she said lightly. "And—"

"It's *not* yours," Mick protested. "I'm not shirking my duty, I swear."

"I didn't mean—"

"Plenty of single parents manage not to raise juvenile delinquents."

"I…" Kayla's hand slipped off his to wrap around her mug.

"Hey, don't look so glum," he said. "I'm not going to mess this up. I made myself a promise years ago that I'd be a lean, mean parenting machine and I'll be damned if I break my word to myself or let down my kids."

Kayla shoved back her chair and headed for the coffeemaker. She hesitated with her back turned to him, then she slowly spun around. "Mick, you're a great father. Single…or otherwise."

He shrugged off the compliment, aware the crucial years lay yet ahead. "We'll never know about the otherwise, huh?"

She went very still. "I…guess not."

Some note in her voice made him look at her more sharply. He still couldn't fathom her expression, but the sun started streaming through the kitchen window and it caught her hair, setting it to a golden blaze. The sight set fire to his blood, and his mind went back to that phone conversation they'd had before Jane's fateful tromp down the stairs.

The nights have been lonely for me, too, Mick. Come home. Come home and let's be company for each other.

He'd assumed the mood was spoiled, but he was thinking of her again, naked, that sunny hair wrapped in his fists, her sleek skin warming beneath his mouth. She was standing in that spot, he realized, that enchanted spot on the hardwood floor that she'd occupied the moment of their first kiss.

The noise of his chair legs scraping backward was loud, but not as loud as the sound of his heartbeat in his ears. His weariness drifted away as he walked toward her. She stood her ground, her blue eyes as wide as the sky in the window beyond her.

Should he say something—what?—because surely she read what he desired on his face. He wanted her and how she could make him laugh and smile and need like a man—and not just a father—lightened all of his burdens.

She didn't move as he approached. When he cupped her face in the palms of his hands, her lashes brushed her cheeks and her body swayed toward him. "On my way home from school, I promised myself I'd make up for my daughter's rudeness," he said.

Her soft laugh washed over him like more sunlight. "Is that what you call this, Mick?"

"No. I was planning on making you breakfast."

Her lashes lifted and his heart stuttered as their laserlike color hit him. "So it's scrambled eggs or sex?"

The teasing note in her voice lightened things even more. "Whatever you want," he said, then bent over to take her mouth, his tongue slipping inside to paint the slick surface just inside her lips, before surging forward to slide along hers.

Her body flowed against his. Smiling to himself, he put an inch of air between their mouths. "Bacon or more *besos*?" They'd learned that *beso* meant *kiss* in Spanish when they'd traveled with the kids to Baja, California, one year.

Her fingers clutched the cotton of his T-shirt. "I'm not sure you're playing fair."

"I'm just as happy to play dirty," he whispered. "Listen to this deal—orgasms now, omelets later. What do you say?"

She winced. "The alliteration is well…atrocious."

He laughed, feeling the last of his tension drain away. The sad things he'd seen on his shift, the worry he'd walked into when he'd caught Jane arguing with the nanny; they both evaporated as he caught Kayla closer against him. "But what do you say, honey?"

"I say…" She looped her arms around his neck.

"I say, take me to bed, Mick, and we'll concern ourselves with later...well, later."

It wasn't only fatigue and problems that dissipated
in Kayla's room, though. Mick felt the years drop
away, too. He was young again, the sensation of a
woman next to him almost brand-new. His chest
tightened as he unbuttoned her top and he saw her
breasts swell over the cups of her bra. His thumb
found the already-hard tips, and that was like a mir-
acle, too.

"You're beautiful," he said. "You want me."

"Well, duh," she said, laughing at him, as she at-
tacked the snap of his jeans.

They fought each other for supremacy then, each
determined to get the other naked. He ended up pick-
ing her up and tossing her onto the mattress, then following her down to get the job done. But she shifted,
straddling his hips so that their jeans were pressed
together and her sweet breasts bounced into his range
of vision.

He skated his palms up her sleek back and jack-
knifed forward to catch a nipple in his mouth. Sucking strongly, he felt her response through two layers
of denim. She wriggled against him, her damp heat
against his rigid erection. When he switched to lick
the other nipple, she moaned and he yanked at her
button and zipper, loosening her pants enough so he

could run his hands beneath them and her panties. His hands cupped luscious curves as he pressed his hips upward, giving her the friction she needed.

"Mick." Her reedy voice had him moving again, switching spots with her so she was on the bottom and he loomed over her slender figure. With a sweep and tug, he had her naked. "Oh, God," she whispered as he bent low to take her mouth and his knee pressed into the juncture of her thighs.

"I want to make you feel good," he said, then slid his mouth along her cheek to her ear. "I want you to come in my hand and in my mouth and then I want to come inside you."

She shuddered. "We need to get your clothes off, then."

"My intentions are good, but my will is weak," he said. "I think I'll keep my pants on until we've completed step one and step two of my plan."

She protested, and even tried tugging at his hair, but firefighters could be single-minded when they had to be. While he loved her touch anywhere on him, he ignored it as he scooted down on the mattress. He ran his tongue around one areola, playing with the silky and wet folds between her legs.

She was swollen there, open for him already, and he took her with two fingers, then drew them out to paint them over the rigid nub at the top of her sex.

Kayla made sounds, sweet, sweet sounds, and he used them as his guidebook to her pleasure.

Indirect pressure and fast rhythm there, strong suction and the edges of his teeth here. Thank God he'd kept his pants on, but even then he was pressing hard against her lean flank, his own pleasure tightening, tightening.

She broke with a cry and he clamped down harder on his needs. *For Kayla, for Kayla, for Kayla,* he chanted in his head, and when her tremors calmed, he slid lower, pushing up and outward on her knees.

"Oh, my God," she said, her fingers clutching weakly at his hair. "I can't."

"Just try," he whispered, then blew air against that pink, glistening skin. She twitched, and then again as he breathed onto her pretty flesh a second time. When his tongue touched down her hand fell to the bed.

She tasted creamy-salty-sweet and he took her flavor into his mouth over and over and over, his tongue flat, his tongue flickering, his tongue telling her how lovely she was for sharing this with him in a soft rhythm and in a hard-driving pulse.

"Mick..." Her voice was breathless. "I can't..."

He knew how to coax. Kids on bicycles. Dogs from drainpipes. Frightened people from twisted metal. "Sure you can," he said. "I'm right here. I'll catch you. C'mon, Kayla."

And then she did come. And he held her quaking hips in his big hands and felt higher than he did when he'd climbed his first extension ladder as a rookie so many years before.

Her sated expression did nothing to diminish his desire. As he shucked the rest of his clothes, her half-drowsy eyes watched him like a cat content in the sun. But when he kissed her again, she went from drowsy kitten to wide-awake feline, rubbing against his naked skin, kissing his chest, his belly, his—

"Whoa, whoa, whoa," he said, lifting her away from there.

She pouted. "You're supposed to be making me feel good. That was making me feel good."

"And me too good," he murmured, flipping her yet again, then donned the condom he'd put on the bedside table. When she opened to him, her arms, her legs, he didn't hesitate again.

His body surged into hers.

He felt powerful. Wide-awake. And so damn young. Energy coursed through his veins and he was nothing like the overburdened father who feared the future any longer. He was a man on the brink of a new day—one he was looking forward to living.

Kayla's hips moved up, into his, and then she was

drawing his head down, taking him into a kiss that sizzled like a shooting star—and shot him right out of orbit.

They dozed. After the night he'd had, he was surprised he even roused when she moved.

"Where're you going?" he said, his voice slurred.

"I have a lunch date," she replied, but he heard it from far away. He didn't like the idea of her leaving, but sleep beckoned. Kayla wasn't really leaving him, he thought, as the tide took him back out. He'd fulfilled his plan and made her feel so good that surely she wouldn't ever go away.

"I'm so glad you could join us today. We've always enjoyed your company *so* much," Patty told Kayla with enthusiasm after they were seated at the café table. Then she cast a sidelong, guilty glance at her husband, Eric. "Okay, okay. I know I promised not to lay it on too thick."

Eric Bright, a lean man with short blond hair and wire-rimmed glasses, shook his head at his wife, though the corners of his mouth twitched. "Really, Kayla, thanks for coming. How's Mick?"

She thought of him now, as she'd been trying not to since she'd left the house. He'd been on his belly, his face buried in the pillow, the breadth of his shoulders and the long shallow valley of his spine exposed by the sheet bunched at his hips. A tingle rekindled inside her remembering everything that had led to his drowsy state. A flush rose up the back of her neck, so she took a swallow of her ice water to cool herself.

"Tired today," she managed to say. "I gather that last night they had to go out on more than one tough call."

Eric nodded. "And Lee and Jane?"

"Lee's good." Then she shrugged. "Jane's fine, too, but sixth grade..."

"Oh, don't I know." Patty rolled her eyes. "I was dreading fifteen, but eleven going on twelve has hit our family pretty hard. Danielle wanted to wear eyeliner to school today."

"Jane, too." It helped to hear that her charge wasn't the only girl with wild ideas this morning. "She wasn't too happy with me when I told her to change her clothes and wash her face."

"Wasn't too happy" was an understatement, of course. She'd been furious, and Kayla got upset just thinking about it. They'd butted heads from time to time, but the girl usually saved her moments of rebellion for her father—and now she had more sympathy than ever for what Mick's future might hold.

"I figure I'll get the cold shoulder until Dani needs

something at the mall or wants to have her friends over," Patty said.

Her husband groaned. "I must have been in the shower and missed this altercation entirely—for which I am eternally grateful."

Patty reached over to pat his cheek. "You'll pay when it's time to talk to our son about safe sex."

"He's only eight years old!" Eric protested.

"And when the time comes, you'll be repeating yourself until he's eighty-eight or married and out of the house, whichever comes first."

The waitress arrived to take their orders, then went away when they made clear they hadn't cracked their menus yet. The many-paged binder affair could take a whole hour to peruse, Kayla thought. She wondered if she'd make it back before Mick left her bed, and she didn't...

Don't think about that! she told herself. Nor did she want to think about that vague undercurrent of disquiet that had been running at the back of her mind since Mick had returned from taking the kids to school.

With a smile, she glanced up at the couple. "What are you two planning to have?"

Patty flipped a couple of laminated pages. "Eric, you're going to go for the eggplant parmigiana sandwich, right? Or maybe you feel like the patty melt?"

His eyes bugged out behind his glasses. "They have patty melts? You are the goddess of menu minders," he told his wife with sincere appreciation. "I didn't even see a patty melt or an eggplant parmigiana sandwich and I've been staring at this thing as long as you have."

Patty looked a little smug as she shot a glance at Kayla. "I always find exactly what he wants."

"It's a division-of-labor thing," Eric told Kayla. "She's on the lookout for my perfect lunch, I make sure she keeps her cell phone charged."

"Seems fair," she said. But it seemed more than that, it seemed sweet, and she enjoyed the thought of the couple looking out for each other in even those small ways.

"You and Mick probably have unspoken agreements like that, too," Eric said. "You make the coffee every morning, he regularly checks the oil in your car."

"It's not exactly the same," his wife pointed out. "Kayla's not Mick's wife, but his kids' nanny."

"Meaning Patty will check your oil *and* make the coffee every morning if you agree to go with us to Europe."

"Hey!" his wife frowned. "I thought you forbade me to arm twist. Kayla already said she was ninety-nine percent sure she was staying with the Hansons."

Ninety-nine percent? Kayla thought. Was it really wise of her to dismiss the offer so quickly? After that unpleasant scene with Jane that morning and then Mick's unsettling comments before they'd made love, she just wasn't so sure anymore.

Their orders were taken; their meals arrived. Kayla asked questions about their planned stay in Europe and listened intently, but studied the pair's interaction with equal care. They moved in a rhythm that she liked, that she recognized. She and Mick were similar in some ways, easily moving about the kitchen or packing the car for a trip, aware of each other's moves and depending upon each other's expertise.

Mick was a whiz at getting everything in the trunk. Kayla was the one to make sure everyone had a sweatshirt in case the day turned cold.

But Patty and Eric had more. Where she and Mick avoided physical contact, the other couple were easy with each other in that way, too. She brushed a crumb off his shirt. He fed her a seasoned French fry that came with his patty melt. What would it be like to have that with someone?

When Eric turned to the dessert menu, she excused herself for the ladies' room. She was surprised that

Patty didn't go with her—it was customary, in her experience, to make the trip with the other female in the party—but then she figured that the couple would take the few minutes to discuss her.

They'd outlined the duties of the nanny they were looking for. The possibilities for solo and family travel had been presented. A salary even mentioned. She imagined Patty turning to Eric now and asking, "Is there a chance that she'll leave Mick and Jane and Lee?"

Was there a chance? Kayla pondered the question for herself as she headed back toward the table. Before she'd come up with a solid answer, her cell phone buzzed in her purse. She pulled it free and looked at the screen. Her mother.

"Mom?" she asked. Her mother's calls were rare and even rarer was it to hear from her midday. She was a busy executive's assistant from eight-to-five who then went home to a bustling house filled with her husband and three active high schoolers. "Is something wrong?"

Karen Collins sounded relieved. "You took my call."

"Ye-es?" Kayla frowned. "And you're surprised because…?"

"I forgot your birthday." She hesitated. "Tell me your father didn't forget, too."

"I had a nice celebration luncheon with my girl-friends," Kayla said, skipping over the direct answer. "And then Mick and the kids surprised me with cake and balloons and really great presents."

Her mother groaned. "Oh, honey. I'm so sorry. Can you forgive me? Mitzi had a debate tournament that weekend and Doug Junior was doing something or other for Scouts. Not to mention that Annie had that 4-H—"

"I get the busy family thing, Mom, no problem," she said, ignoring a pang of sadness.

"It's a problem! Yes, I realize your friends stepped in and that your employer acknowledged your day, but you should have had something more. Your mom and your dad at least wishing you the best. And—dare I say it—a date."

"I had a date."

"You did?" Her mother sounded so eager.

Kayla swallowed her groan, wishing she hadn't mentioned it. "It was no big deal, but yes, I had a date."

"Tell me about him!"

She could see the table and Patty and Eric now. Her feet slowed. The couple were laughing together over something, their hands entwined. It was beautiful how they were so relaxed together, yet still so obviously attracted. They were a solid, comfortable unit that still gave off love sparks.

It was what she wanted. It was what she couldn't have with Mick.

"Kayla?" her mom prodded. "About your date?"

"It was nothing," she said slowly.

Or, to be more precise, it wasn't going to come to anything. For whatever reason, Mick had implied more than once that he didn't want a woman in his life on a permanent, intimate basis. She'd been trying to ignore that fact. Wishing it away.

But after her episode with Jane—*you'll never be my mother!*—and then his declaration this morning—*plenty of single parents manage not to raise juvenile delinquents*—she had to face the fact that Mick saw himself as a solo lean, mean parenting machine. In that case, he and the kids would never be hers in that real way she wanted.

She didn't think anything less was good enough for herself now, though. That was what had been running through her head since she'd left Mick in her bed. She'd told him during the early phone call not to worry about her—that she could take care of herself—and it was time to do just that.

She had to see the truth that Mick didn't want to commit, and after a lifetime of being forgotten or overlooked by family, she needed commitment. She wanted family.

And if she had to tear herself away from one to find her own…so be it.

With new determination in her step, she returned to join Patty and Eric.

Chapter Eleven

Kayla had been tossing and turning in her bed for a couple of hours when she heard her bedroom door pop open. Even horizontal, her stomach dipped. Mick?

She rolled her head on the pillow to see a slight figure outlined in the doorway. "Jane?" She lifted to an elbow. "What's wrong? Don't you feel well?"

The girl hesitated, then she ran toward the bed. "I want to make things right."

Relief washed through Kayla, making her almost giddy. "Me, too," she said, leaning to flip on the bedside light. For two days, the members of the Hanson household had been tiptoeing around each other with exaggerated politeness. "Come here."

In her soft yellow pajamas, Jane climbed into the bed as Kayla scooted over so the girl could have the spot she'd warmed on the mattress. With the child tucked under the covers, Kayla dared to brush her dark hair from her forehead. "Is something going on at school?" she asked.

"I have that book project due next week," Jane said. "I don't know where to start."

Jane was notorious for putting off tasks she dreaded. Lee would tackle the assignment he most disliked—spelling—first, but his sister procrastinated until the deadline breathed down the back of her neck.

"Remember our strategy for that?"

"Break the project into smaller pieces," Jane said. "Focus on the first and not worry about the next until that one's finished."

"Right. So when you're ready tomorrow, we can sit down together and separate the whole into manageable chunks."

"I did finish reading the book," the girl said, brightening. Then her face fell. "Because Dad wouldn't let me watch television after dinner. He said maybe I was learning my rudeness from my favorite shows."

"I'm sure you can earn back the privilege," Kayla said.

"That's why I'm here."

Kayla's brows rose. "To get back your viewing quotient of *iCarly*?"

Both Jane's lashes and her voice lowered. "Not really. I don't like that I hurt your feelings."

Kayla blinked away the sting at the corners of her eyes. "Something tells me that I might have hurt yours, too."

Jane wiggled a little in place. "If only you would let me wear makeup. Just a little…"

She stopped as Kayla was already shaking her head. "It's your dad's rule," she reminded the girl.

"You could ignore it. Or you could tell him it was wrong."

"No, because I happen to agree with him. But the fact is, Jane, that even if I didn't agree you were too young for lip gloss and mascara, I'm the nanny and he's the father. Which means he gets to make the rules and I'm paid to help you follow them."

Something flashed in the girl's eyes. "He pays you to take care of us."

"True." Was that what was bothering her? "I do get a check for taking care of you." She tapped Jane's nose with a gentle fingertip. "But the caring *for* you and Lee comes from me, free of charge."

Tears welled in Jane's eyes. Kayla froze, then scooted closer to gather the girl close. "What is it?" This didn't feel like making things right. This felt like things going in the wrong direction. "Why are you crying?"

One fat drop spilled down Jane's cheek. "How could you care for us and plan to leave us at the same time?" she accused.

Kayla's face stiffened into a mask. She hadn't known how and when to broach the subject of the Brights' proposal and so had become as dedicated a procrastinator as Jane. How had the word got out? "What exactly are you talking about?"

"The other night…the night before I tried to go to school in Maribeth's clothes, Danielle said she overheard her parents. That they think you'll go to Europe with them and be their nanny."

"Oh. Well." That explained Jane's outburst, she thought, remembering the girl's impassioned *Go away and stay there!* that had occurred even before her lunch meeting with Patty and Eric Bright. "I hadn't talked to Danielle's parents about that."

"So it's not true?"

Kayla hesitated. She couldn't flat-out lie. "I hadn't talked to them about that yet," she amended. "Since then, they did speak to me about the possibility."

"So are you? Are you leaving us?"

Kayla sighed. "Oh, Jane." Where did this sit on the right-wrong spectrum? She hugged the child tighter to her, running her hand over her hair as she'd done a thousand times before. Her chest ached, brimming with maternal feelings that weren't hers to have.

The children weren't hers.

Their father wasn't hers.

"Don't you love us?" Jane asked, her voice sounding closer to five than eleven.

"Of course I love you," Kayla said. "How could I not love you?" But was assuring the child of that so wise?

Because it all felt so wrong now. She shouldn't have stayed for six years. Six years of wiping tears and spills, of packing lunches and suitcases, of wrapping owies and Christmas gifts…those six years had cemented the family into her heart.

But nothing cemented her to them in return.

"You'll go to college in seven years, Janie," she said, rubbing her cheek against the child's hair. "Lee in ten. How old will I be then?"

Jane sniffed. "Thirty-four when I go. Thirty-seven for Lee. Old!"

"Yeah. Old. Maybe too old for some of the things I want for myself." A husband. Children who belonged to her.

"I want you to stay with us forever," Janie declared, squeezing her tight.

"But *you* won't stay forever," Kayla pointed out. "College, remember? And then you'll have a job and an apartment and maybe a husband and your own kids after that."

Sighing, Jane tucked her head tighter to Kayla. "Sometimes I don't ever want to grow up."

"I know," she said, closing her eyes. "I know the feeling." But she'd been playing house for six years and it was past time for her to grow up, too.

The girl grew heavy against her. "Let's get you back to your bed," she whispered, then half led, half carried the child up to her room, her heart heavier than Jane's slender form.

As if she was still small, Kayla arranged a stuffed menagerie around the girl's drowsy body. Then she leaned down and kissed her on the brow. "Don't let the bed bugs bite."

Jane's hand crept out to clasp Kayla's wrist. "Do you have to go?"

She didn't mean right now. She meant away from them. Her free hand covered Jane's fingers as she searched inside herself for how to put things right. For what *was* right.

She thought of Ellen Hanson and the promise that she'd made to her just a few days before. She'd promised not to let her children down, and wasn't part of that being a role model for Ellen's offspring? A woman who hung on to hopes and didn't seek what she needed in life—love and family of her own—wasn't a good example for either Lee or Jane. To make things right—for all of them—it seemed clearer and clearer that she'd have to move on.

"I think I do, Jane," she whispered when she saw that the girl had fallen asleep. "I think I have to leave all of you."

She turned to the door, jumping when she saw a large shadow looming there. Her hand reached for her thudding heart. "Mick," she whispered. "What?"

He beckoned, and her nerves still jangling, she obeyed. In the hall, he reached around her to shut Jane's door, then, still silent, he pressed her against the wall and bent to take her mouth.

The kiss demanded her cooperation. She clutched at his naked shoulders—he was wearing only pajama bottoms—and opened her mouth to the thrust of his tongue. Her skin had cooled on her trek through the house in her oversized nightshirt, but now it was hot, burning, set on fire by Mick's mood.

It would be so easy to go under, so easy to surrender to skin and kisses and good sex, but none of that changed the fundamental conflict between them. She pushed him away.

"I want more," she said, her chest heaving.

"I'll give you all you want."

But she noticed he didn't move. She noticed his hands were at his side, his fingers curled into fists. Mick understood what she'd meant.

Running his hands through his hair, he turned away. "Do you really have to go?" he asked, in an echo of his daughter.

If she wanted to make things right, she really did.

Mick was in a foul mood the morning after his hallway encounter with Kayla. She was going to leave them, head off with Poaching Patty and her family to Europe to find adventure and everything he and the kids didn't have to offer her here.

She'd be visiting the Eiffel Tower while the only tower around the Hanson household was the tower of dirty towels that needed to be washed each week. Her day would be filled with exotic foods and handsome men instead of PB and J and an eight-year-old with a newfound ability to fart with his armpit.

Then there was Mick himself. A guy willing to share her bed, but who knew he didn't have the energy or the ability to make her happy as well as keep up with the rest of his life as fire captain and father.

No wonder she was leaving them.

But he was going to be gracious about it, he decided as he stopped at the elementary school close to the lunch period. Today the PTA was sponsoring a midday safety fair. He was on tap to provide a mouth-to-mouth resuscitation demonstration. Kayla would be there helping out. No doubt that traitor, Patty Bright, would be on hand, too.

Yet he wasn't going to let the impending change in his circumstances affect how he went about his day. No sour grapes or surly attitude on display.

"What are you looking at?" he barked at a little kid as he walked through the school gates with the life-size demonstration dummy.

The child's eyes rounded and he clutched his lunchbox to his chest. "What'd you do to the person?"

Mick realized he was carrying the mannequin with both his hands around its neck. He eased his strangling grip and softened his voice. "It's not a real person. We practice on it to save lives. Come see me after you eat your lunch and I'll show you."

The kid made a face. "My lunch is tuna fish. It tastes gross."

"You can breathe tuna fumes into Donald Dummy's face. That'll be fun."

The boy's interest kindled. "How about if I eat my carrots and cookies instead?"

A familiar voice piped up beside Mick. "Christopher Carter, I think you better eat everything in your box. Then you'll have enough energy for math after lunch."

Mick glanced over at Kayla. Her hair was pulled back in a golden ponytail and she wore jeans, a fuzzy white sweater and low-heeled suede boots. He wanted to take her home and snuggle with her on the couch.

He'd settle for taking her home and chaining her to the couch.

Instead, he cocked his head toward the little boy. "Pal of yours?"

Her gaze was on the youngster whom she waved to as he took off in the direction of the lunch benches. "I run a math recovery group that meets once a week. That guy's always claiming he's too tired to remember his times tables."

His eyebrows rose. "I didn't know about this."

"It's new. Once I got my degree in early elementary ed, I approached the principal about putting it to use. It's a mixed bag of kids who could use some extra help. I meet with them the last forty minutes before school ends on Wednesdays."

Just another thing she'd be leaving behind when she went on her search for adventure. "Where do I set up?" he asked, his voice abrupt.

She didn't comment on his brusque tone of voice. Maybe he was a better actor than he thought. Maybe he could really be gracious about all this.

He had a table in the auditorium. Beside him, the nutritionist for the school district set up a food pyramid. On his other side, the school nurse positioned little bottles of hand sanitizer to give away. The plan was for the event to be more casual than formal. The kids would be allowed to roam around the space and stop and ask about what interested them.

Not that he was trying to unfairly attract his share of the crowd, but he'd also brought turnout gear, including boots and a helmet, for the kids to try on if they wanted. Not to mention his other ace in the hole. He went back to sprucing that up when he heard a little voice behind him.

"It's Mrs. Thompson!"

Christopher Carter, with or without fish breath, had arrived on scene. He was staring at the dummy laid out on the table. "You made the dummy look like our principal."

A little firefighter's trick he'd picked up along the way. Nothing tickled kids more than to see a lifeless mannequin wearing a wig that resembled the hairstyle of their head administrator, along with a school T-shirt, a flowered skirt and the woman's ubiquitous walkie-talkie in a fake rubber hand. He grinned at the boy. "You want to learn how to save her life?"

"I don't know. She says no tag on the blacktop."

"No tag? That does sound a little harsh. Maybe she'll have a change of heart if you give her mouth-to-mouth."

The kid stared. "Eew. Gross."

Mick sighed. There was always this hurdle to overcome. "Maybe I should have dressed up the mannequin like somebody else."

Christopher Carter's smile turned sly. "Maybe. Maybe like her." His gaze shifted to the auditorium entrance, where Kayla was shepherding in a group of little ones. Kindergarteners, he guessed, because they had that special wide-eyed look and a couple of them were holding hands unselfconsciously.

Mick cast a look at Oak Knoll Elementary's little Lothario. "So you like Ms. James?"

The kid's expression said *duh*. "Don't you?"

His gaze went back to the blonde. "Yeah. Yeah, I do."

She was leading a group of the teeny ones around, pointing out the different displays. Hunkering down, she helped a little girl unbutton her sweater and then tied it around the kid's small waist. Mick had seen her do things like that for kids—his kids—dozens of times. But this time it made him catch his breath.

She wasn't just the nanny, or the hot sexy thing in black boots whom he'd taken to bed.

She was so much more: a gentle touch, a teasing laugh, a patient teacher, a kind friend. A woman who was walking out of his life.

He had to look away as she walked toward him now. "Captain Hanson," she said, a gaggle of kindergartners around her. "This is some of Room 2."

A five-year-old pointed toward the rubber figure. "Is it dead?"

"No." He didn't bother to explain it was dressed as the principal. Apparently his little joke was beyond the ken of kindergarten. "This is not real. It's a dummy— "

"Bad word," a gossamer-haired cherub said, frowning at him. "We don't call anybody a dummy. It's a Room 2 rule."

Mick's gaze met Kayla's. She shrugged, her amused gaze clearly letting him know he was on his own. Like he'd be, forever, after she left.

He glanced back at the little girl. "I'm sorry. It's a...like a doll. And we practice on it to save lives."

"So it is dead," the first kindergartener reiterated.

"I..." He gave up. "In a way, I guess you're right." Shaking his head a little, he moved over to the table and launched into his supersimple spiel about exchanging the breath of life. Whether the contingent from Room 2 got anything out of it, he didn't know. Not after he wound down and looked up, straight into Kayla's eyes.

Under his hand he felt the rubbery exterior of the dummy. It was just how he'd felt after Ellen's death. Lifeless. Emotionless. Stiff. But then time had passed and he'd heard his children laughing again and seen the sunshine in the hair of the pretty woman smiling at him over coffee every morning. Somewhere after grief and before Kayla going away he'd...

He'd fallen in love with her.

He'd fallen in love with her!

She gathered her charges around her now, a puzzled expression on her face, and herded them away while he just stood there, still as stupid as that dummy, because it had taken him so long to realize the truth.

How long had he been living with her and loving her? When had *wow* crept into the room with them? Not just the *wow* of sexual attraction, but the *wow* of...wow, she's it.

She's The One.

"Oh, that's just plain unfair," a new voice said.

Mick jerked out of his reverie to see freckled Patty Bright, her gaze on the turnout gear he'd brought. "What?"

"And an instant camera to take pictures of the kids wearing this stuff, too, ensuring yours will be the most popular station. I had no idea you were such a cheater, Mick."

He frowned at her. "It takes one to know one," he muttered.

Her gaze sharpened. "Excuse me?"

"Nothing." He recalled his promise to be gracious. But God, that was even more difficult now, knowing that Patty had lured away the woman he loved. Knowing he couldn't do anything about it because he had only those dirty towels, his testing daughter and his boy with the armpit farts to stack up against the call to adventure that came from the Brights. And because, bottom line, he still didn't believe that despite these feelings he had for Kayla, that he had the emotional vigor to take on the burden of her happiness on top of Jane and Lee's.

Not only must he put his children first, he couldn't, wouldn't, put Kayla last.

"Mick?" Patty came forward, concern on her face. "What's wrong?"

"Not a thing. You won." It was more growling than gracious, but hey.

"Won what?"

"The nanny, of course. My nanny." *My Kayla.*

"Mick," Patty said. "You're wrong. She turned our offer down."

He blinked. "She turned you down?" But last night she'd made it clear she was leaving. "Whose nanny is she going to be, then?"

"I don't know." Patty shrugged. "She said she thought it was time she made a change, but she didn't want to get so entwined again with someone else's family."

"What's she going to do, then?" he wondered aloud.

Patty shook her head. "I got the sense that she was considering leaving childcare altogether."

A thought that didn't put Mick in any better of a mood. If she wasn't seeking adventure in Europe, then why was she leaving them? Why couldn't she stay? Last night she'd told him she wanted "more" and he'd thought she'd meant the excitement of travel. The glamour of new possibilities on a new continent. But if it wasn't that…?

Screw gracious, he thought. Screw pretending he was in a better mood. He was going to get to the bottom of this.

Chapter Twelve

But Mick couldn't get the answers he wanted when he wanted them. He didn't catch sight of Kayla after his conversation with Patty at the safety fair. Then he had a meeting to get to and then he had to return to school for the kids. Once home, he remembered the nanny had her girls' night out scheduled with her crew from We ♥ Our Nanny. She'd already left for her friend Betsy's.

So he went through the father motions. Homework. A little basketball in the driveway with Lee. He started dinner and even went to work on creating a clean tower of towels by folding what he found in the dryer. Through it all he felt as if he carried a thousand-pound weight on his chest.

I might as well be a hundred and four. I feel that worn-out.

"Daddy, what's the matter?" his daughter asked him after dinner. They were in the family room. He was seated on the couch, but the kids were standing, eyeing him instead of the TV. Oh, yeah, he'd forbidden Jane to watch her shows for a few days.

He sighed. "You can turn it on, kids," he said, gesturing toward the screen. "Surely Zack and Cody or Phineas and Ferb are going about their zany business."

Neither child moved. Then Lee glanced at his sister. "Are you having a bad day, Dad?"

Mick tried to smile. "Yeah, buddy. I guess you could say so. But don't worry about it."

"I do worry about it." Lee launched himself forward, and snuggled in right next to Mick's side. "Tell me what to do. I can help."

Mick smiled again, this one more natural. He heard the echo of himself in his son's words. "Thanks, Lee. But I'm good."

"You're not good, Daddy." Jane found her place on the free cushion next to him. "Lee's right. We can do something for you."

He wrapped an arm around each of them, pulling them closer. "Just sit here with me a few minutes."

Closing his eyes, he let his head drop back and took in the warmth of his children pressing against him. As he blew out a long breath, he felt some of his tension ease. They were good, his kids. Holding them helped.

The ache in his heart was still sharp. It killed him to think he'd fallen in love with the nanny only to watch her walk away from him, but he'd survive. The kids would lighten the weight of it.

The kids would lighten the weight of it.

His eyes popped open. He looked down at his beautiful children and the way they'd rallied to him. The way they were cuddled up to him right now, adding their strength to his.

Oh. My. God. The kids would lighten the weight of everything. Meaning, Mick realized, that they weren't a burden on his emotional foundation, but a buttress to it. This was the magic he hadn't understood. It went way beyond Disneyland. Together, they were a team. And "together" meant he wasn't alone in ensuring the family's health and happiness. He should have known that. Seen that sooner.

He cleared his throat, new optimism filling his chest. He'd been a short-sighted dummy, but he'd been given the breath of life just in time. God, he hoped it wasn't too late. "Kids…about Kayla."

Jane looked up at him, her dark eyes solemn. "She thinks she has to leave us."

Lee shot upright. "What?"

Mick squeezed his son's shoulder. "I've got an idea about that." A hope about that. It gave him new energy and he pushed to his feet, a grin breaking over his face. "I think you two are going to approve." Forget a hundred and four. He was a young man with a plan to get his woman.

Although the night was cold, Kayla felt completely comfortable under a patio heater and beneath a soft old quilt on the tiny space behind her friend Betsy's little cottage. It was detached from her employer's house and adjacent to the neighbor's spacious backyard. Kayla took a sip from her wineglass and noticed a male figure pass through the sliding glass doors at the rear of the big place next door.

"Is that him?" she whispered to Betsy.

The other woman nodded. "The crabby one. The smell of charred flesh is the giveaway."

"Ew," Gwen said. "Do you have to speak of grilled beef in that manner? There's nothing wrong with a man who likes to barbecue."

"There's something wrong with this one. I am definitely not fixing him up with anyone I know. He's taken to calling me Boopsie."

Gwen and Kayla glanced at each other. "The twins call you Boopsie."

"Exactly. So I don't know why you guys want to keep talking about him. Sure, he's handsome and everything. Not to mention that hard body of his. But he's disagreeable—hello? Crabby!—and I need a third four-year-old in my life like I need a hole in the head."

Kayla decided against pointing out no one said anything about Mr. Crabby getting *into* Betsy's life. Who was she to comment on someone else's business? She was in disentangle mode.

Gwen swiveled to gaze at Kayla again. "Your life hasn't been going smoothly either, I hear?"

"Huh?" Kayla frowned. "I don't know what you're talking about."

"Patty Bright came to me about her family's posting to Europe. She said she tried to persuade you to be their nanny."

Betsy gasped. "You're going to Europe? You're going to leave Mick and the kids?"

She didn't want to say that out loud. "No, I'm not going to Europe, Bets. That didn't seem to be the right step for me."

Gwen lifted an eyebrow at their hostess. "How about you, Betsy? Not that I encourage my nannies to play hopscotch with their positions, but it *is* a wonderful opportunity. Several months overseas, plenty of off-time for solo travel…"

Betsy looked down at her wine, then her glance stole across the fence to the house next door. "I'm not much of a solo girl. And my boys need their Boopsie."

"All three of them?" Gwen murmured, for Kayla's ears only.

Kayla hid her own sad smile. If she left town, she might miss the previously unscheduled but clearly upcoming adventures of Boopsie and Mr. Crabby. It wasn't a happy thought, but she'd come to realize that by filling her life with other people's families and other people's relationships that she was missing out on building her own.

It was just that Mick and the kids felt so much like her own!

"I'm leaving them," she said abruptly. "I'd appreciate it, Gwen, if you'd come up with some ideas for a new nanny for Jane and Lee."

Betsy stared at her with round eyes. Gwen took the news more calmly. "Is anything wrong? Is there something I should know about?"

"Nothing's wrong. Oh, I'm having a little trouble with Jane and lip gloss, but nothing unexpected. At heart she's such a warm and generous girl, and Lee is the same. The hardest thing about caring for him is keeping him in socks that don't have holes."

She felt her eyes begin to sting, so she focused her

gaze into the distance. "You'll find someone perfect for them, won't you?"

"What about Mick?" Gwen asked. "Is he difficult to work for?"

"The opposite." She waved a hand. "Easygoing. Pitches in wherever he's needed. Not demanding."

"But he's a problem for you," Gwen said.

Kayla shook her head. "No. No."

"All right," Gwen agreed, in her calm voice. "So then we should be looking for a new position for you. You don't want the Brights. You want to leave Mick and the kids."

She never wanted to leave Mick and the kids.

"I can't be a nanny again," she said, setting down her wine. "I'm no good at it."

Betsy scooted forward on her chair. "Don't say that, Kayla. You know you're fabulous at what you do. Best nanny ever!"

"No." Kayla was shaking her head again. "Worst nanny ever."

Gwen cleared her throat. "Kayla—"

"I broke the cardinal rules," she confessed, closing her eyes. "Betsy, you called it out weeks ago."

"Kayla—"

"I think of the kids as my own. And I've fallen in love with their daddy." She covered her face with her hands. "It's a disaster."

"Umm…"

"A disaster, I tell you," Kayla said.

Then, big, warm hands pulled hers away. She opened her eyes and there Mick was, his dark hair, his rangy build, the brown eyes that she'd seen grief-stricken, amused, hot with desire. Now there was tenderness in them and…?

She didn't know. Tugging against his hold, she tried to get away. "I made a mistake—"

"Nope. That would be me," Mick said, yanking her to her feet. "Now say goodbye to your friends."

He already had her halfway across Betsy's tiny patio. Wreathed in big smiles, they were both shooing her along. "He's a much better choice than Mr. Crabby," Betsy called out.

A disgruntled voice floated from the yard next door. "I heard that, Boopsie."

Once in the car, a mosquito whine started in Kayla's ears. It only got louder when Mick slid behind the steering wheel. "What—"

"Hold the questions until we get home," he said, shooting her a little smile. "Please?"

"But—"

"I made a promise to the kids that I'd get you back as fast as I can. If we start into this now…I don't know when we'll make it."

"Still—"

"I left them alone, Kayla. I know we're only five minutes away, but who knows what might happen. Jane could hide Lee's Pokémon game and he could say she smells like onions—"

"Pickle burps."

"Huh?"

"It's pickle burps." And then she shut her mouth and tried to tamp down her curiosity, her embarrassment and even that little sprout of hope that was struggling to surface inside her. Mick had witnessed her confession—*I'm in love with their daddy*—and he hadn't gone running for the hills, but that didn't mean...

She couldn't let herself believe it meant anything at all.

Then they were pulling into the driveway and then they were walking into the house. She heard the patter of footsteps on the floor and Mick's hand was at the small of her back leading her into the dining room. It was just like the day before her birthday: balloons, a cake, confetti strewn across the table.

"Surprise!" Jane and Lee yelled together.

She took in their excited faces. "Something's going on," she said. "Did I fall asleep and wake up a whole year later just in time for another birthday party?"

Lee bounced on his toes. "It's not your birthday, La-La. Dad realized it's your anniversary."

"*Our* anniversary," Jane corrected, grinning. "It's the anniversary of the date you first came to be our nanny."

She shifted her gaze to Mick. He shrugged. "What a coincidence."

What a crock, but she couldn't squelch the kids' excitement and there was something thrumming in the air when she looked at their father. Something newer than the sexual tension that she'd experienced before, but that was there still, too.

He gestured to the stairs with his thumb and nodded at Jane and Lee. "Scram."

They giggled and ran, then both ran back to Mick. Their hugs brought a new sting of tears to Kayla's eyes. He rubbed his big palm over both their heads. "My good luck charms," he said, then pushed them on their way.

Over her shoulder, Jane met Kayla's gaze. "Welcome home," she said.

Okay, the hope was really starting to flower now, but Mick was just staring at her, saying nothing. God, she didn't want to presume and then have this all wrong. Her eyes went back to the cake on the table. It read "Happy Birthday" in loopy letters of red frosting.

Putting her hands in her pockets, she pretended to

inspect it carefully. "They didn't have one that said Happy Anniversary?"

"To be honest, I didn't ask. This one seemed more appropriate." He came up behind her. She could feel his body's warmth just an inch from her back, but she forced herself to stand straight instead of leaning into him.

As if he read her mind, his big hands closed over her shoulders and pulled her into the cradle of his body. His head lowered. "I want this to be a birthday of sorts, Kayla. I want this to be the birthday of the real family I want to make with you."

Had he really said that? Or was it just her overactive imagination? But she could feel his heart thudding between her shoulder blades. He smelled of that scent she'd bought him for Christmas. The bright colors of the cake and balloons in front of her were impossible to overlook.

Okay, this must be real.

"Mick." Her voice sounded husky. Too full of emotion. She cleared her throat because she had to be certain about what he was asking of her. "You wouldn't say that...do this...because the kids, you, me, we have a routine that works—"

"No." His fingers tightened on her. "I respect you too much for that."

"Respect?" She closed her eyes. That sounded like

what she promised herself she wouldn't do—settle. "Respect isn't enough, Mick."

He spun her around. "Honey. What I'm trying to say is that I'm not asking you to be a chauffeur for the kids or a cook for the family or even the laundry lady. I want a lover. A wife. For me."

Yes. *Yes.* She flung herself against him and threw her arms around his neck. Their mouths found each other and the kiss was hot and possessive and certain.

Still, she pulled away, just far enough for air. "Are you absolutely certain? Because—"

"I love you, Kayla," he said, his forehead pressed against hers. "Don't you feel the *wow* in the room? You're The One. My One."

Kayla felt that silly telltale sting of tears again and she squeezed her eyes tight. He pressed his mouth to her cheek, her chin, her temple. "Am I too late?" he whispered.

She shook her head, and he drew her against him once more, enfolding her in his arms. "I worried I might be too late," he said.

"What took you so long?" she asked, her voice watery.

"I was all upside down in my thinking," he admitted. "I thought that if we were together, that it would make me responsible for your happiness—"

"I'm responsible for me, I told you that."

"Yeah, well, we first-responder types are notorious for believing the world won't turn unless we have control of the wheel." Then he loosened his hold so he could see her face. "But you've got a blind spot nearly as big as mine, honey, because we're better when we're willing to lean on each other when necessary. We're better together."

Together. She loved the sound of that. But…

"I started remembering all that we've shared over the years—from worrying about the kids' colds to panicking over the missing cat. It finally got through my thick head that our love would be a partnership, not a responsibility. That we—all of us—make each other stronger." He gave her a gentle shake. "So you're not on your own either, sweetheart."

"Together," she said, nodding.

"Right. We'll work together to make each other happy and our lives good. The kids are part of that, too." He smiled. "So…please, go ahead and give up being the nanny."

She swallowed. "And?"

"Take on the job as my wife and Jane and Lee's mother?"

Before her mouth could open, a train of sound came roaring down the stairs. Clattering footsteps, hoots and hollers, then the exuberant presence of two grinning children. Mick looked at them with a rueful smile. "Didn't I ask you guys to stay away until I gave the signal?"

Jane ignored her father's admonition. "Can I go with you to shop for rings?"

Kayla looked at the two children who so long ago had been taken into her heart. But did that go both ways? "You guys understand? You're on board with this?"

Eyes shining, Jane nodded.

Lee jumped up and down. "Hurry up and say yes, Kayla," he urged. "Me wants cake."

Her gaze met Mick's. "On his wedding day," they said together.

Then she drew Lee's dad down to kiss his mouth. "On *our* wedding day."

His eyes closed, his arms tightened. "Is that a yes?"

"It's a yes," she said, kissing him again, out of the corner of her eye, noting the curious cat was sitting on a chair, batting at a balloon. Then she pulled both kids into their circle of family. "And a yes," she added, kissing the top of Jane's head. She squeezed Lee as he wiggled closer. "And a yes."

Her tribe. Yes, indeed.

* * * * *

SPECIAL EDITION®

COMING NEXT MONTH
Available October 26, 2010

#2077 EXPECTING THE BOSS'S BABY
Christine Rimmer
Bravo Family Ties

#2078 ONCE UPON A PROPOSAL
Allison Leigh
The Hunt for Cinderella

#2079 THUNDER CANYON HOMECOMING
Brenda Harlen
Montana Mavericks: Thunder Canyon Cowboys

#2080 UNDER THE MISTLETOE WITH JOHN DOE
Judy Duarte
Brighton Valley Medical Center

#2081 THE BILLIONAIRE'S HANDLER
Jennifer Greene

#2082 ACCIDENTAL HEIRESS
Nancy Robards Thompson

SSECNM1010

REQUEST YOUR FREE BOOKS!
2 FREE NOVELS PLUS 2 FREE GIFTS!

SPECIAL EDITION
Life, Love and Family!

YES! Please send me 2 FREE Silhouette® Special Edition® novels and my 2 FREE gifts (gifts are worth about $10). After receiving them, if I don't wish to receive any more books, I can return the shipping statement marked "cancel." If I don't cancel, I will receive 6 brand-new novels every month and be billed just $4.24 per book in the U.S. or $4.99 per book in Canada. That's a saving of 15% off the cover price! It's quite a bargain! Shipping and handling is just 50¢ per book.* I understand that accepting the 2 free books and gifts places me under no obligation to buy anything. I can always return a shipment and cancel at any time. Even if I never buy another book from Silhouette, the two free books and gifts are mine to keep forever.

235/335 SDN E5RG

_____
Name   (PLEASE PRINT)

_____
Address   Apt. #

_____
City   State/Prov.   Zip/Postal Code

_____
Signature (if under 18, a parent or guardian must sign)

Mail to the Silhouette Reader Service:
IN U.S.A.: P.O. Box 1867, Buffalo, NY 14240-1867
IN CANADA: P.O. Box 609, Fort Erie, Ontario L2A 5X3

Not valid for current subscribers to Silhouette Special Edition books.

Want to try two free books from another line?
Call 1-800-873-8635 or visit www.morefreebooks.com.

* Terms and prices subject to change without notice. Prices do not include applicable taxes. N.Y. residents add applicable sales tax. Canadian residents will be charged applicable provincial taxes and GST. Offer not valid in Quebec. This offer is limited to one order per household. All orders subject to approval. Credit or debit balances in a customer's account(s) may be offset by any other outstanding balance owed by or to the customer. Please allow 4 to 6 weeks for delivery. Offer available while quantities last.

Your Privacy: Silhouette is committed to protecting your privacy. Our Privacy Policy is available online at www.eHarlequin.com or upon request from the Reader Service. From time to time we make our lists of customers available to reputable third parties who may have a product or service of interest to you. If you would prefer we not share your name and address, please check here. ☐

Help us get it right—We strive for accurate, respectful and relevant communications. To clarify or modify your communication preferences, visit us at www.ReaderService.com/consumerchoice.

SSE10R

HARLEQUIN®

A Romance

FOR EVERY MOOD™

Spotlight on
Inspirational

Wholesome romances
that touch the heart and soul.

See the next page
to enjoy a sneak peek from
the Love Inspired® Suspense
inspirational series.

*See below for a sneak peek from
our inspirational line, Love Inspired® Suspense*

*Enjoy this heart-stopping excerpt from
RUNNING BLIND
by top author Shirlee McCoy,
available November 2010!*

**The mission trip to Mexico was supposed to be an
adventure. But the thrill turns sour when Jenna Dougherty
and her roommate Magdalena are kidnapped.**

"It's okay. I'm here to help." The voice was as deep as the
darkness, but Jenna Dougherty didn't believe the lie. She
could do nothing but lie still as hands slid down her arms,
felt the rope around her wrists.

"I'm going to use a knife to cut you free, Jenna. Hold
still."

The cold blade of a knife pressed close to her head before
her gag fell away.

"I—" she started, but her mouth was dry, and she could
do nothing but suck in air.

"Shhh. Whatever needs to be said can be said when
we're out of here." Nick spoke quietly, his hand gentle on
her cheek. There and gone as he sliced through the ropes on
her wrists and ankles.

He pulled her upright. "Come on. We may be on
borrowed time."

"I can't leave my friend," Jenna rasped out.

"There's no one here. Just us."

"She has to be here." Jenna took a step away.

"There's no one here. Let's go before that changes."

"It's dark. Maybe if we find a light…"

"What did you say?"

"We need to turn on the light. I can't leave until I know that—"

"What can you see, Jenna?"

"Nothing."

"No shadows? No light?"

"No."

"It's broad daylight. There's light spilling in from the window I climbed in through. You can't see it?"

She went cold at his words.

"I can't see anything."

"You've got a nasty bruise on your forehead. Maybe that has something to do with it." His fingers traced the tender flesh on her forehead.

"It doesn't matter *how* it happened. I'm blind!"

Can Nick help Jenna find her friend or will chasing this trail have Jenna running blindly again into danger?

Find out in RUNNING BLIND, available in November 2010 only from Love Inspired Suspense.

SHLISEXP1110

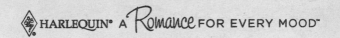

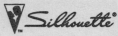